At the end

Jay Cook

iUniverse

AT THE END

iUniverse books may be ordered through booksellers or by contacting:

iUniverse
1663 Liberty Drive
Bloomington, IN 47403
www.iuniverse.com
844-349-9409

ISBN: 978-1-6632-5634-8 (sc)
ISBN: 978-1-6632-5633-1 (e)

Library of Congress Control Number: 2023917590

Print information available on the last page.

iUniverse rev. date: 09/15/2023

Dedicated to my mom. Thank you for being my best friend, my rock, my shoulder to cry on and my biggest fan, always. You truly are the most amazing woman I have ever known, and I am honored to call you Mom.

Prologue

When people thought of the end of days, the apocalypse, it seemed to be the common opinion that it was inevitably going to occur, as nothing lasts forever. The beliefs upon how this would befall them varied, however. Some ideas made logical sense, others, very little.

Some people believed that a disease of some sort would wrack the planet, wiping out civilization in one fell swoop. Chemical warfare was also an option. Others thought that global warming would cause the planet to flood itself, slowly and efficiently snuffing out all forms of life.

The largest consensus was another asteroid crashing into the planet. That would surely do the trick. The most radical of thought felt something more like a zombie apocalypse much more exhilarating.

The truth of the matter was, they were all wrong. When the end did occur, not a single person was prepared, despite centuries of speculation. When it came, it came swift and thorough. Although, those that lived in those dark days would have said that it lasted forever. Days upon days of endless panic, fear, horror and loss.... Only at the end was the truth revealed and it was a truth so unimaginable it bordered on idealistic.

Chapter 1

The day started out like any other for twenty-five-year-old Manhattan resident, Jenny Lowe. She woke to sunlight streaming through her sheer curtains, casting her bedroom in a warm glow. Early morning traffic could be heard through the windowpane with muted beeps and rumbles. The rich smell from her preset coffee maker permeated the air.

Jenny appreciatively inhaled the intoxicating aroma and rose from her bed. Raising her long arms and arching her back, she stretched her lithe body. With delicate fingers, she brushed back tendrils of light brown hair from her face.

Pushing the curtain aside, she glanced out the window. It was early November and despite the barrenness in preparation for the upcoming winter months it had been unseasonably warm for the past week. Light sweaters were worn in the morning and quickly cast off as the day progressed.

Curiosity settled, she released the curtain and grabbing her robe from the end of her four-poster mahogany bed, she headed toward her small kitchenette. Briefly, she paused in front of her recently unoccupied guest bedroom. Hearing no sounds of stirring, she continued and poured herself a large mug of coffee.

Looking around her small kitchen, she noted the subtle changes that had occurred in the last few months. The sunflower yellow walls were still bright as ever, but now carried small fingerprint smudges that refused to disappear no matter how much she scrubbed them. Her cow cookie jar had been removed from the table and tucked back into the highest cabinet. Toys lay stacked in a pile in the corner of the room. Where there had once only been one chair set at her small kitchen table, there now sat two.

Her condo had been used purely for functionality. She had been content with the most basic, never feeling the need to embellish the place. Now, however, her place of convenience had been morphed into a home.

Five months ago, her parents had died in a tragic car accident leaving her the sole custodian of her four-year-old brother, Nathan. Nothing could have prepared her for the sudden loss or her new role into parenthood.

It had not been an easy transition for either sibling initially. They often butted heads while learning each other's nuances. Tempers flared quite frequently in the early days and Jenny discovered the hard way that a 4-year-old came with a larger than life set of lungs, much to the aggravation of her neighbors. However, over the last few months, they had settled into a routine that suited them both.

Mornings were a repeated series of coffee, dressing them both, breakfast at the diner a few blocks away followed by playtime in the park. Jenny had quickly discovered that Nathan had an abundant amount of energy to burn off after the sleepiness of the night wore off.

Afternoons were devoted to Jenny's work on the novel she was writing while cartoons played quietly in the background. Nathan was particularly fond of Sesame Street and Mickey Mouse Club, which suited her just fine. She liked that they were educationally stimulating as well as a source of entertainment.

During the evenings, Jenny would help Nathan tie on his apron, and he would "help" her to make dinner. This was often followed by board games or cards. Then, when Nathan started to yawn, he was put to bed, and her novel writing resumed until exhaustion claimed her as well. Her days were considerably longer since his arrival, but very rewarding.

Steam rose from Jenny's mug as her thoughts turned affectionately toward the little man who had taken up residence in both her home and her heart. Before he had moved in, they had not been overly familiar with each other. In truth, prior to her parent's untimely deaths, she had only seen him a time or two. Knowing him as she did now, she felt a pang of regret for the lost years.

The estrangement with her parents had begun years ago after a dispute over Jenny's chosen career path. Her parents did not support her dream of being a successful author and felt that a steadier career was the only option.

They were determined to force her into college with the goal of a high-powered career in mind. In their eyes, her work was a hobby to be indulged in after "real career" hours. Jenny did not see it that way and since then her dream was realized, several times over. The seed of dissention had been planted early on and firmed when she quit college and moved to Manhattan, New York.

As a child, and even into her adult years, Jenny was a shy, introverted person. However, when she began learning to write, she discovered a passion for it. When she was writing, she could be whoever she wanted to be, and the feeling was freeing. Her passion for writing knew no bounds and brought her a kind of happiness she could find in little else. In her books, she was animated, spirited, and brave. She could be all that she wanted to be and more. This was a thing that her parents could not seem to understand.

Waitressing jobs had seen to her needs until her passion for writing finally paid off. She had quit her job then, found her condo in Manhattan and lived quite comfortably off the royalties from her creations.

After years of success, the rift between parents and child had remained. Despite her successful career, even in the end, they could not comprehend her point of view.

Considering their views of their own parental failure, she was surprised at the birth of her younger brother 21 years after her own birth. She doubted that the relationship between parents and child had been any better of an experience for him. Even still, after their deaths, Jenny felt a familial responsibility toward her brother.

Nathan could be described as a tremendously active, goofy and sometimes mischievous little man. With his white-blonde hair and deep blue eyes, he had an almost angelic appearance. Upon looking at the child, one would never guess that he had a tendency toward playful antics.

Nathan's pranks did not seem limited to occasional peanut butter in her sneakers, a frog in her pillow or honey on the door handles. He had a knack for mischief and was highly creative in his endeavors.

Despite his mischief, or perhaps demonstrative of, he had an undeniable air of intelligence about him. He was also quick to smile and laugh, which was quite infectious.

He was small for his age but lean, giving him a lanky appearance despite his height. His little face still held traces of baby fat and he looked a bit like a cherub. He was undoubtedly one of the most adorable children she had ever seen. Yes, she thought to herself, that brother of hers was something else.

"Sissy?" A small, sleep-filled voice called from behind her, "Is it time for breakfast? My tummy is grumbly." Jenny turned and eyed her brother with mirth. Nathan's hair was tousled, some bits sticking straight up as if he had stuck his finger in a light socket. He let out an indelicate yawn, remembering to cover his mouth at the last second.

Jenny nodded with a smile. "Yes, Booger." She replied affectionately.

"Let's go get dressed so we can feed your grumbly tummy. We have got to do something with your hair too!" she said with a laugh and she reached out and tickled the little imp before ushering him toward the bedrooms.

In Nathan's bedroom, Jenny helped him select his outfit for the day making sure to include a thin bright orange sweatshirt which he balked over but relented in the end. Getting him dressed was a quick affair.

Moving into the bathroom, they attempted to tame the mess that was his hair. After running a brush through it, it was quickly apparent that it was not going to cooperate. In the end, they wound up soaking it and the front of Jenny as well. The matter settled, Nathan departed for the living room, flopped down on the couch and turned on the tv while Jenny went to change out of her wet clothes.

"I'm going to need to buy some kid-friendly pajamas." Jenny said to herself as she deposited her sodden silk pajamas into the hamper. She hung her robe on the hook on the door and hoped that it would dry by nightfall. Grabbing jeans, t-shirt, a light sweater and a pair of sneakers, she quickly changed and rejoined her brother.

Having dressed for the day, Jenny and Nathan left their third-floor condo, took the stairs and headed in the direction of their usual diner. Unusually quiet, Nathan appeared to be deep in thought. Holding hands, the duo walked in silence, their shoes crunching the dry leaves on the sidewalk.

Other pedestrians passed them, looking down at their phones, oblivious to the world around them. Others appeared as though they were talking to themselves, blue tooth headphones the only evidence of their sanity. It was saddening to Jenny, their dependency on their devices when a whole world surrounded them unseen.

"Sissy?" Nathan's sing-song voice questioned as he swung their joined hands.

Jenny looked down at him curiously. "Yes, Booger?"

"What's a 'nado?" he asked.

Puzzling at his question briefly, not understanding the word used, she responded. "Do you mean a tornado?"

He nodded in affirmation, and she considered how to answer in a way that a four-year-old would understand.

"It's when wind goes real fast around and around, and it gobbles up everything in its path. Just like Cookie Monster with cookies. Why do you ask?" She demonstrated her best Cookie Monster imitation with an "om nom nom!"

"When you were getting dressed, I turned on the tv and every channel was saying 'nado." He replied with a shrug and a grin at her impression. She could be funny when she tried.

"That's odd." She replied as they paused at the crosswalk. She wondered at the reason for the coverage and then dismissed the thought.

Chapter 2

His question forgotten by both; Nathan hurried forward to press the crosswalk button. For good measure, he poked it a few more times. He let out a giggle at the feel of the rubber depressing. And Jenny could not help but grin at his enthusiasm. Seeming to correspond with his mischievous personality, he appeared to find an odd joy in pushing buttons. Elevators and crosswalks were a delight to the boy.

The sign on the pole across the street gave the go-ahead with a beep and a flash. They crossed, Nathan with a renewed bounce in his step. They arrived at the diner a few minutes later and Jenny ushered Nathan to their usual booth before sliding into the seat herself.

Ron's Diner appealed to Jenny for its "mom and pop" atmosphere. There, the staff was friendly and treated each customer as if they were family or very close friends. The waitress' ability to place each person's name to their face was admirable. In this establishment, there were no strangers.

The décor was old fashioned and devoid of any new high-tech gadgets. The tried and true being the theme. The booths had wears and tears attesting to the popularity of the establishment throughout its existence. It oozed an air of comfort and relaxation and had often brought seeds of inspiration to Jenny as she pondered the direction of her latest novel. Pre-Nathan, she could be found there for hours typing away on her laptop.

Looking around, Jenny spotted her favorite waitress, Miranda, behind the old linoleum counter and gave her a nod of recognition before turning back to her brother. "Ready for some breakfast?" She asked. He nodded eagerly and then promptly ducked under the table to hide in his "fort" as he called it.

Miranda was a fortyish, slight woman with flame red hair that tended to frizz into curls that bounced when she strutted about the diner. She had a bubbly and outgoing personality and often had a joyful gleam in her bright crystal green eyes. Laugh lines were etched on her face, evidence of years of good humor.

An immigrant from Ireland, she had an Irish lilt to her voice that was inviting to even a stranger and made the shiest of people comfortable in her presence. Grown men, women, and children alike responded to her as bees to honey. She was simply magnetic.

Not excluded from the group was the owner of the diner, Ron, who fell in love upon first laying eyes on her. The couple had been married for several years and he appeared to take her "fan-club" in stride. Upon meeting Nathan for the first time, she had formed an instant kinship with the boy, much to Jenny's delight.

Ron appeared to be Miranda's opposite. He was a large man in height and girth, standing well over a foot over his partner. He was soft spoken, shy and tended to keep to the kitchens where he felt most comfortable. He was the name to place, but Miranda was most definitively the face to the establishment and the obvious cause to its continued success.

Grabbing the pad from the pouch of her apron, Miranda hurried toward them, not even slowing. She wrote down their anticipated order and tucked the pad back into place. Seeing this, Jenny grinned and supposed they had become predictable in their routine. Miranda reached them in record time, excitement evident in her expression.

"Good morning, you two! The usual, I assume?" She rushed out her pleasantries, unusual for her typical behavior, and then continued without pausing. "Jenny! Have you seen the news this morning? Tornadoes have been popping up all over the world since last night! I thought it was a hoax of some sort at first... You know, like crop circles and such. But it is broadcasting on every network! It's *amazing!*"

"All over the world? You have to be kidding me!" Jenny exclaimed. "I don't know if amazing would be the word that I chose. Tragic maybe. But Nathan did mention it on the way over here. He asked me what a 'nado is. I hadn't turned on the television yet today, so I wasn't aware."

At the sound of his name, Nathan resurfaced and sat back down, a sudden and perfectly behaved gentleman.

"Will we see a 'nado?" Nathan asked wistfully.

Miranda grinned at Nathan. "What a clever boy you are! Sorry, but I doubt a tornado will get anywhere near here. We haven't seen one in years and it was nothing to spit on." She said with an affectionate pat to his head.

Nathan leaned into the caress like a kitten searching for one more pet.

To Jenny she replied, "I'm sure you *could* come up with a better description. How is the new book faring?"

Jenny grunted in mock frustration. "It goes… at a snail's pace lately. I'm having a hard time with the chapter that I'm on. It seems like the revisions are never-ending. I just can't seem to get it right. I know where I want it to go but…" She let out a sigh.

Miranda patted her hand and replied with confidence. "You'll get it. And it will be just as great as the last one, I'm sure. I couldn't put it down! I told Ron when your next book comes out, we should buy a boatload and sell them here and maybe convince the author to do a signing? Wink, wink. Anyway, let me put this in and I'll be right back with your coffee and of course, a chocolate milk for the growing boy here."

With a wink to Nathan, she rushed off to place their order.

"Nathan," Jenny asked as she turned to her brother. "Do you know how to do the spoon trick?" She slid two spoons across the table for them.

"Spoon trick?" he asked, immensely curious, and bouncing on the bench seat.

"Yes. If you huff on to the spoon, you can make it stick to your nose." She replied and then demonstrated; her spoon now dangling off the end of her nose. Nathan gave it a few ineffective tries before finally succeeding himself.

Pride gleaming in his eyes, Nathan smiled at his newfound skill and they both turned carefully as Miranda returned with their drinks. She had a good hearty, musical laugh at the sight the pair made with matching spoons on the ends their noses.

"You two!" She chuckled. "I would have expected that from the boy, but you too, Jenny?" Miranda admonished, and Jenny shrugged, looking unabashed and perhaps a little proud.

"It's a very big accomplishment that every child should master." She replied.

Nostalgically, Jenny thought of her own childhood

when her father had taught her that trick and briefly wondered why it had not been passed down to her younger sibling. In truth, it was one of her fondest memories, despite their later rift.

Jenny remembered sitting in a diner like the one she was in, around Nathan's age, and her father sitting there, spoon on nose, while using an authoritarian voice, telling her that she needed to spend more time working on her spelling. In truth, he had no idea that he had inadvertently guided her onto the path that she was on, one he had disagreed to so much.

Another customer entered the diner and Miranda rushed off to take his order with her usual animated flair. Jenny admired and sometimes envied her for her flamboyant and bubbly personality. Minutes later, Jenny and Nathan's breakfast arrived, and they quickly polished off their plates of scrambled eggs, toast and home fries, extra grease, charge free.

With full, contented stomachs, Jenny and Nathan waved goodbye to Miranda, having settled their bill with a hefty tip for their favorite waitress. Then, they set out for the park across the street from the diner. 'Nados" were a distant memory, pushed to the back of their minds.

The park was not overly large, spanning only two city blocks. It had large grassy areas, clipped short and well maintained. Park benches were scattered throughout the perimeter and squirrels weaved between them collecting whatever scraps they could find. Pigeons, also in attendance, cooed as they competed for their own share of the tasty morsels. The ambiance was soothing, laid-back and comforting for all ages.

There were two sets of swings, one on each side of the park. Trees scattered haphazardly throughout, nearly barren of leaves in preparation of the upcoming winter months. The best feature of the park, however, was a very old tree located in the center of the park.

The tree was enormous in girth, its large, thick branches looked like arms reaching for the sky, as if to pluck a cloud from the heavens. The tree's main feature was a fair-sized hole close to the ground. It was a source of fascination to the local children. Often it was used as a hideaway during their bouts of hide-and-seek.

It came as little surprise that the hole happened to be one of Nathan's favorite seclusions. Nobody knew the true age of the tree, but it was rumored to be in the hundreds, perhaps thousands of years.

The park was a little more crowded than usual this day, due in part to the warmer climate. Children ran around gleefully as still-waking parents watched cautiously from the benches; travel mugs filled with coffee or other forms of caffeine clutched in their hands. A few elderly people took up residency on the unoccupied benches; their newspapers open, reading glasses perched precariously on the tips of their noses.

Once they reached the soft grass, Nathan looked to Jenny expectantly, a plea in his eyes to be released from his sister's care. Jenny nodded and with a whoop of delight, he jetted away, heading for the group of children near the swings. Jenny ambled after him looking for a spot in the grass that she could sit and observe from.

"Stay where I can see you!" She called after him. He nodded in affirmation, not stopping in his mission to join the crowd of laughing children.

Finding a comfortable spot, Jenny sat and stretched her legs out in front of her. Plucking a blade of grass from the ground, she rolled it in her fingers and watched as a game of tag soon erupted.

Giggles and laughter filled the air as the children darted about randomly in an attempt to avoid being tagged from the "it" child. Nathan nimbly evaded, his small, lean stature providing him an advantage.

The "it" child was larger than the rest and a bit heavy set. Sweat was already trickling off his face and his shirt clung to recently developed damp areas. He panted as he ran, doggedly determined to catch his prey. Jenny had to admire his determination. He stomped after the other children, arms outstretched, seeking a morsel of skin to end his quest.

Another child was finally tagged, and the game resumed. Jenny's attention wavered and she looked about the park; not really focusing on anyone or anything particularly. It was then that she happened to glace back at the diner and spotted a gentleman rushing from the establishment in obvious distress. She sat up straight, perked her ears and struggled to hear his pleas.

The man was red in the face and was hollering toward the park goers, his hand pointing toward the sky. But his words were lost to the echoes of the children playing. Looking in the direction of his pointed hand; two realizations hit Jenny. The first was that the sky was suddenly darkening. The second was that the implausible was about to hit Manhattan. A tornado was coming.

Chapter 3

"Tornado!!! Run!!!" The man's voice finally reached above the crowd of park-goers and children.

Off in the distance the sky was black; startling in contrast to the clear skies that had been above them in the park minutes ago. Suddenly, lightning flashed, and a deep rumble shook the ground. All around, panicked screams erupted, adult and child alike in an eerie chorus, and a riot immediately ensued. Parents raced to retrieve their dumbstruck children, and they ushered them away to seek the nearest shelter.

In the flurry of people running this way and that, Jenny lost sight of Nathan. Panic gripped her and she struggled to breathe over the lump that formed in her throat. She struggled to her feet and screamed for him. "Nathan! Where are you?" No reply was given and for a moment, she stood frozen in fear. "Nathan!"

Jenny's body unlocked and she raced to the spot that she had seen him last. She spun in panic-stricken circles, her eyes searching desperately for some sign of him. Spotting a shock of white-blonde hair about twenty feet in front of her, she ran to the child, calling out for him.

"Nathan! Over here!" But the child did not respond, standing still as a corpse staring at the sky in awe and unabashed fear.

She grabbed the child by the shoulder and began to spin him toward her when she realized that it was not Nathan.

"Leave my son alone!" A woman yelled from behind her before knocking into Jenny, forcing her to the ground.

In her haste to flee, the woman inadvertently kicked Jenny in the temple. The pain was instantaneous.

Jenny struggled to maintain consciousness, but she could feel the darkness consuming her. Her last thought was that she desperately needed to find Nathan. She couldn't fail him! At that, her body went limp, impervious to the chaos surrounding her.

Jenny lay there prone to the elements before a loud rumble awoke her and the ground shook beneath her body. She had no idea how long she had lain there. The sound filling her ears was so deafening, it was as if she were laying on the tarmac of the airport. Struggling to her feet, she saw a large conical cloud sweeping its way closer. Debris swirled around the mass before being discarded and tossed haphazardly.

She stared, frozen in fear and watched helplessly

as the cone split, once and then again. Suddenly, one unbelievable tornado turned into 4, splitting off and heading in different directions of destruction, one of them heading directly toward her, as if it sensed her growing fear and panic like a wolf to its prey.

She screamed, but the sound did not reach her ears. It was whipped away by the growing, howling winds. Lightning crashed in the sky and rain pelted and drenched her in an instant. Looking about wildly, she looked for a place for shelter and saw a bit of orange fabric sticking out of the hole in the large tree. Hoping beyond all that she was, she raced to the tree, convinced she had at last found her missing brother.

Relief flooded her as she spotted a face peering out from the tree and realized that she had indeed located her brother's hiding spot. Briefly, she considered whether she would be able to get them both to safety before the tornado arrived, but soon discarded the idea. There simply wasn't enough time. That decided, she sprinted toward the tree to join him, the wind whipping at her, slowing her progress.

Jenny peered into the hole before squeezing in, gauging its size. Crawling inside, she clutched Nathan close, thankful to have found him unharmed. It was a very tight fit inside the tree and although she could stand, she was forced to bend herself around his body. She maneuvered herself so that only her lower back and rump were exposed, using her own body as a shield to protect her brother. She would hold this pose even if it killed her, literally.

In the darkness, Jenny could barely make out Nathan's features. What little she could see broke her heart and she wished she could protect him from his fears. Tears streaked down his face and his lip trembled. He clung to her shirt as if she were his life preserver in the middle of a tumultuous sea, which was not unlike the actual feeling of the current event.

She had never been a praying kind of person before, but in that moment, she offered thanks for locating her precious brother and a plea for their safety. She vowed to herself that if they survived this nightmare, she would pray every day without fail; she would give up caffeine; she would never write again; she would do *anything* if they could be spared.

Although it hardly seemed possible, the roar outside of their sanctuary climbed to extraordinary levels. It was as if the Earth itself was screaming in protest. The wind at her back whipped at her shirt, stinging her flesh as it slapped against her.

"Oh my God.. Oh my God... Oh my God.." Jenny whimpered, her prayers suddenly a terror-filled loop.

Nathan burrowed closer and she could feel his small body shudder against her. Her own limbs echoed the sentiment.

Suddenly, the tree groaned and shifted as it began to

lean. A silent scream stuck in Jenny's throat and in her terror, she wondered if these were their last moments. The air seemed to be sucked away, leaving them gasping for breath. The roar outside of their tree rose to impossible heights, intensifying their terror. Time seemed endless as they awaited their fate.

The tree rocked again leaning further over and the pull at Jenny's back increased. She braced herself with her shoulders and legs, forcing her frame to inhabit as much space as possible for fear they would be sucked out of their haven. Her muscles screamed in protest, but she held on. Just when she thought she couldn't hold on any longer the storm began to relent.

Outside of their sanctuary, the roar began to quiet, and the wind slowed to a gentler tempo. The tension left Jenny's body and swallowing back her own tears of relief, she held Nathan close as he wept. For long minutes, they continued to stand in their tree, waiting for some assurance that it was indeed safe to leave.

When Nathan had cried out every tear his four-year old body could manage to muster, he hiccupped, wiped his face into Jenny's shirt and looked up at her with swollen eyes.

"Jenny? Is it all done?" he asked in a wavering voice.

"I think so." She replied in an equally shaky voice. "I'm too scared to look."

Nathan nodded agreement at her statement, and they

stood in the silence, listening for long minutes. Jenny's limbs felt like limp spaghetti and her mind raced with thoughts of what had just occurred.

"Nathan, why did you hide in the tree? Why didn't you come to me?" she asked, her tone soothing despite the turmoil she felt inside. "I couldn't find you and it scared the hell out of me."

"Everybody started screaming and running and I got real scared," He replied in embarrassment. "I didn't want to get runned over, so I ran to the tree."

Jenny nodded as if in understanding, but inside she shuddered at the thought of what could have happened to the little boy had she not found him. She pushed the thought aside and, deciding it was indeed safe now, attempted to climb out of the tree.

Disentangling herself proved much more difficult than the climb in, but after some moves that would make the Cirque De Soleil proud, she managed to at last touch ground again. She turned, grabbed Nathan's hands and helped him next.

Jenny closed her eyes for a moment as if mentally preparing herself for what she knew was a sight that would scar her for life. She had seen the aftermath of a tornado on television before and knew that it would be horrendous. She did not want to look. Not really.

Inwardly calling herself a coward, she opened her eyes. Television did not do it justice. Not even close. Even in her artistic mind, there were no words for the desolation surrounding them. Her mouth hung open as her brain attempted to process the scene before her. Blinking did not erase the chaos, despite her fervent desire for it to be so.

Gone was the beautiful park that Nathan had played in. It was as if exiting their tree, they had stepped into another world completely. Nothing was recognizable. Where there had been carefully cultivated grass there were now mounds of dirt, broken boards, bricks, trash and upturned cars. The tree itself was partially uprooted and now leaning, where it had stood proudly before.

There were large, thick tufts of smoke, fire and building materials where buildings had busily lined the streets. Very few people could be seen emerging from wherever they had taken refuge. They wandered about, seemingly aimlessly, as shell shocked as Jenny and Nathan felt. The scene around them was scarily like a zombie horror flick.

A tiny hand slid into Jenny's palm as if seeking comfort, had there been any to give. She tightened her own fingers around them and looked down to Nathan's dirt caked face.

With the protection from the tree, it amazed Jenny how utterly filthy Nathan was, and could only imagine how bad her own appearance was. Nathan looked like he had been dragged through a pile of dirt and the only pink left on his face were from his tear streaks. His hair meticulously doused and combed just this morning stood on end. His appearance might have been comical had this been any other situation.

"Can we go home, Sissy?" He asked hopefully.

"I hope so." She replied hesitantly. "If there is a home to go to. This looks pretty bad…"

She trailed off while contemplating just that. Just this morning she had worried about her robe drying before bedtime, now she worried if they *had* a home anymore!

Hand in hand they crossed the park, crisscrossing their way around the mounds of destruction. As they neared the street, Jenny observed the sign for Ron's diner hanging from the heap that was now nothing but a tarnished, but fond memory.

Jenny's heart hurt at the sight of her beloved diner in such disorder. Gone was the entryway with the cliché dinging bell. The booths were scattered and hardly recognizable. They had been torn from their bolts and tossed about, a sign of the strength of the tornado. Kitchen accessories joined the mad heap, a stove here, dishwasher there. The sight was utter madness.

The sound of weeping on "the side" of the building caught Jenny's attention and despite the foreboding voice in her head telling her she did NOT want to know, she felt compelled to find the source.

Turning the corner with Nathan in tow, she discovered

a very much alive Ron, clinging to something in his hand. His sobs wracked and shook his body which suddenly seemed so frail. Jenny instantly wanted to offer him comfort, not even knowing the source of his pain. Her brain simply could not wrap around what could hurt this man so much until she realized it was a hand that he clung to.

An unwelcome force drew her forward, and as they inched closer, Jenny spotted the most unwelcome sight that would be burnt into her memory for the rest of her life. Standing out amongst the rubble before her was a mass of bright red hair and a very familiar face. Much like a train-wreck, Jenny couldn't look away. Helplessly, she stared into the cold, muted, dead eyes of Miranda.

Chapter 4

A sob wrenched its way free from Jenny's throat before she could stop it. Tears filled her eyes, threatening to spill over. She had not wanted to draw attention to the scene before her, hoping that Nathan would not notice. She couldn't help herself, and Nathan did indeed notice. It was hard not to with Ron's sobs permeating the air.

Jenny placed a gentle hand on Ron's back, silently offering what comfort and condolence she could muster, feeling inside it would never be enough. She wrote love stories, and theirs had been one for the books. Never would she have ended it like this, so tragically, so horrifically.

Nathan tore his hand from Jenny's and raced to Miranda's body. "Miranda!" He yelled, not fully understanding that she would never respond again. "Jenny, help her! We have to help her!"

"We can't help her, Nathan." She said sorrowfully. "Miranda has gone to heaven to be with Mommy and Daddy."

She looked to Ron for assistance, but he did not appear to even recognize their existence. His sorrow was too great, and he seemed to be in a trance of grief.

"But she is here! I can see her!" Nathan yelled, in obvious confusion.

He had not seen his parent's bodies after their deaths, so it was difficult for him to grasp. He patted Miranda's face gently, as if to wake her.

"Please wake up, Miranda." he pleaded.

Ron finally moved, his eyes crazed with grief, and he pushed Nathan away from Miranda, thrusting him into the dirt beside her.

"Don't touch her!" He yelled as he drew a large kitchen knife from the pocket of his filthy apron.

Jenny yanked Nathan to her and shoved him behind her back to protect him and looked into Ron's surprisingly pleading eyes.

"I just want to be with her." he pleaded and without hesitation, drew the knife across his own throat.

A croak escaped her throat as blood oozed from the wound and his last muddy gargle was rendered. His body hit the ground with a thud. Jenny put an arm around her brother's shoulders and, as carefully as possible, attempted to lead him away from the sight.

Nathan once again pulled free, and not even noticing Ron's prone body, ran back to Miranda and gently stroked her hair. A renewal of tears filled his eyes. He looked at

Jenny, his eyes a reflection of the pain and deep sorrow that she herself felt.

"I love her, Jenny. She was always so nice to me. And she'd give me cookies when you weren't looking. She said it was our secret."

"I loved her too," Jenny replied softly. "But Miranda would want us to say goodbye and be happy that she is in a better place."

"He loved her the most," he said in a sad voice, nodding to the now deceased Ron. "Goodbye, Miranda. I love you."

Nathan whispered and then turned and held out his hand to his sister, needing her comforting touch.

Jenny's heart broke for the boy. In the span of 5 months, he had witnessed far more trauma than a boy of his age should.

The pair walked in silence toward their home completely numb to the devastation around them. The "streets" were gone. Third Ave, which they traveled daily to get to the diner was hardly recognizable. To go in the direction that they desired, they were forced to go around, climb over or under mounds of wreckage. This fact did not even register. They were lost in their own thoughts. All they knew was they needed to make it to 88th street where they had resided. Home.

They came to what was left of the crosswalk at 88th street and Third Avenue to find the poles leaning precariously over the wreckage. Nathan raced to the pole, searching for the button in desperation.

Jenny let go over his hand and watched, understanding that this was something that he *needed* to do to hold on to some kind of sanity after the ordeal they had just survived.

Finding the button, he depressed it, and a calm came over him. Once again, he grabbed onto Jenny's hand and looking both directions despite the obvious lack of cars, led Jenny across the way.

As they drew closer to their home, Jenny was filled with apprehension. The desolation and destruction had not ceased during their extended walk. Were they now homeless? Or by some miracle did the condo still stand? Her mind was filled with an endless stream of questions and very few answers. Normally an optimistic person, she felt a hopelessness that was foreign to her. The feeling dug into her heart and clung like a tick to a dog. It was unshakeable.

Minutes later, as they approached 88th street and took the required left, her fears were confirmed. A large pile of rubble sat where their home had once stood. They halted in front of the mound and just stared in disbelief.

Long minutes passed as they stood still as statues. Everything was distorted and it was difficult to distinguish if any of the random items displayed belonged to them or another. There was just nothing evidently salvageable from the mess.

"Where do we go now, Sissy?" Nathan asked quietly, breaking the silence that had once again overtaken them at the sight.

"I don't know. Just give me a minute to think." she replied before sitting cross-legged on the ground. Her legs felt like jelly, and she couldn't *think*. There was just too much to process, and she felt completely overwhelmed.

Nathan turned in front of her and sat in her lap. They drew comfort from each other with their closeness. Silence once again resumed, an unfamiliar and eerie sound considering their whereabouts.

A voice called out from behind them, startling them both, and they turned to see an elderly man approaching them. His words were garbled from his distance. The man moved slowly but nimbly considering he leaned heavily on a long cane. As he drew closer, they could make out his features, and although they did not recognize him, it was a relief to see another seemingly coherent person about.

The man was tall, dark-skinned and very lean. He had an oval shaped face which featured a hawkish looking nose, large lips and a set of dark chocolate eyes. Although his face was extreme in appearance, his eyes showed a look of concern that was endearing.

"Are you two alright?" he asked in a soft-spoken voice as he neared closer. "That's one heck of a lump you have there, miss."

Jenny's hand flew to the large lump surrounding her

temple where the woman had kicked her. In all the chaos, she had completely forgotten about it. In truth, it had not even hurt any more until he had mentioned it. Now it hurt and pounded like the dickens.

"We are alright." Jenny responded with a half-truth. "But apparently homeless now. I was sitting here trying to think of what we can do, where to go now."

The man nodded several times. "Yes, Ma'am. I'm in the same boat. I was heading my way to the 19th precinct. I reckon that would be a good place as any to start. It's not too far of a walk anyway. 20 blocks or so. I imagine the hospital is overrun by now by those that need help, and I don't want to overburden them. I'm still walking on my own two feet. Maybe you and your son would like to join me? Unless you need medical assistance, of course. In which case I would gladly escort you."

Under normal circumstances, Jenny may have had a little giggle over the misconception. But these were not, in fact normal circumstances.

"This is Nathan." she quickly introduced, and polite handshakes rendered. "He's my little brother. I'm Jenny. Sure, we can walk with you to the precinct. I don't think I need the hospital over this little bump." she said underplaying the throbbing in her brain for the sake of her brother's peace of mind. A concussion was a very real fear she kept hidden away to pull out and sorrow over when she had a moment to breathe.

"I'm Reginald, Miss Jenny. Nice to meet you and Mister Nathan. These old bones would be grateful for the company." He replied.

"I don't see a whole lot of us around. Sad day it is. That sure was a doozy. Haven't seen a tornado 'round here since 1974 and it was nothing compared to this. Child's play." he remarked with another head bob.

Quietly, Nathan rose from Jenny's lap and moved toward the remains of the condos. Grabbing what little pieces he could reach, he began removing them, throwing them out of the way. Curious, Jenny accepted the hand Reginald extended toward her and upon standing, went to her brother's side.

"Nathan, what are you doing?" she asked. Intent to stop him before he uncovered another something they did not want to see, she reached for his hand. He pulled away and resumed pulling the pieces, this time with fervor.

"Don't you hear that, Jenny?" he asked frantically and she paused mid-motion to listen.

The sound of a small mewling reached her ears. The noise didn't sound too far and before she could stop herself, she too reached into the mess, trying to get to the source. Inside she was praying that it was not an injured infant. That was a sight that she did not think she could handle. But as they dug deeper, she was relieved with a renewed belief that the source was actually a kitten.

"Did you find someone?" Reginald queried, hurrying over as fast as he could hobble.

"Not someone," Jenny called over her shoulder, "Some*thing*. It sounds like a kitten is trapped under some of this."

She and Nathan continued to remove what they could and at last, a tiny little face appeared.

"Meowwwww!" The kitten whined in distress. A few more pieces removed, and the kitten shrugged itself free of the remaining debris. Nathan reached down and carefully picked it up inspecting it for any visible injury.

"I'm going to call him Lucky." he stated emphatically.

"I don't think it got hurt. Can I keep it, Jenny?" he asked her hopefully. He batted his eyelashes at her and gave her his best puppy dog look.

Since she couldn't see leaving the poor thing to fend for itself and hoping the presence of it would help to distract Nathan from the horrors of the day, she quickly agreed.

"My, my, my-" Reginald said, somewhat in awe. "That sure *is* a lucky kitten! For one so small as that to have survived that tornado… Must not have been on life number nine just yet, I tell ya. Hold it real close, Mister Nathan."

Nathan did as he was instructed, and brought the kitten closer to him, cuddling it to his chest. The kitten responded with a soft purr; its troubles quickly forgotten. With that, Reginald, Jenny, Nathan and Lucky set out for the police station.

Chapter 5

The 19th precinct was 20 blocks away, which under normal circumstances would be a tiring walk, but the destruction around them made it feel nearly impossible. The sun had returned, and with it, the heat, causing an oppressive humidity that was stifling. By the second block, sweat pooled from their bodies and clothes clung to their backs.

Returning to the small group, kitten still securely in his arms, Nathan began to shuffle his feet in impatience.

"Lucky wanted to go fast. He is enjoying the ride." he grumbled.

"Well, Lucky needs to remember that we cannot move as fast as you. We are larger and cannot fit in all of the same places you can." Jenny said as she cleared some of the debris from their "walkway." Nathan's cheeks turned red, and he looked away abashed.

"I'm sorry, Jenny. I'm sorry, Mr. Reginald." he apologized and Reginald wordlessly ruffled the boy's hair.

Hours into their trek and feeling no closer to their destination than when they started, their stomachs began to grumble, and Jenny realized that it had been hours since breakfast. The sun was now high in the sky, a clear indication that it was some time past noon.

"Jenny, I'm hungry." Nathan whined, giving the most pitiful look.

Jenny and Reginald seconded that opinion, and the group began to search for food items in the debris along their way. It was hard to discern anything in the mess, but they had hope. A few blocks more, the sun beginning its descent from the sky, that hope was dwindling fast.

Silently, they trudged along, now at a snail's pace, their eyes searching, when Reginald let out a whoop, startling Jenny.

"That mound over there," he pointed to a large mound to their left, "Is that a refrigerator I am seeing? And some cabinets? Or are my old eyes failing me?"

Jenny looked to where he was pointing and nearly sank to her knees in relief. It *was* a refrigerator, and what appeared to be kitchen cabinets tucked around it. They were high on the large mound and did not look easy to get to, but she would not be deterred from this holy grail. Her stomach growled in anticipation.

"You two stay here," she urged. "It does not look like it will be easy to get to and I don't want you to get hurt. I will climb up there and see if there is anything we can use."

"You be careful there, Miss Jenny." Reginald urged. With a nod, Jenny began to climb, searching for footholds. She had never been the athletic type and she was adding rock climbing to her list of things she never wanted to do after this ascent.

Safe on the ground, Reginald and Nathan hollered encouragement and before she knew it, Jenny had made it to the top. The old refrigerator lay on its side, with the doors facing upward, still sealed. Scooting herself to a more comfortable position, she reached for the handles and pulled.

A blast of coolish air brushed over her face, and she sighed with part bliss, part relief.

"It's still cool!" She yelled down to the pair on the ground, two eyes looking back at her in anticipation.

Jenny peered into the refrigerator and almost groaned in disappointment. She had not expected to find a fine five course meal in there, but the refrigerator was nearly bare. Inside, she found a couple of apples, which she pocketed, some moldy containers that she threw off to the side, and a jar of jelly.

Closing the door of the fridge, she wriggled her way on top and straddled it so that she could reach the cabinets. They were considerably better stocked. Still somehow neatly stacked, she discovered cans of vegetables, canned meat and tuna.

"Did you find anything good?" Nathan hollered up at her.

"A few apples and some canned stuff, but I don't know how we are going to open the cans." Jenny replied, the thought just occurring to her.

Reginald laughed a deep baritone laugh that felt like a balm to the soul considering the previous few hours.

"Never mind that, Miss Jenny. I can open them. Just send them down and we will make us a nice meal to settle our stomachs."

Jenny had not considered the transportation of their treasure and realized she did not have a bag with her and certainly could not carry them down. Her only option was to toss them down the mound and hope that Nathan and Reginald could duck out of the way. One by one, she tossed the cans until they had a nice stockpile stacked at the bottom and the cabinets were bare.

Climbing back down was as much of a challenge as the way up and it took Jenny a long time to do so. By the time she made it to the ground, the sun was already starting to set, and it was decided that it would be too dangerous to continue for the night. They would make camp and resume their journey in the morning.

Reginald and Jenny looked over their stockpile and chose what items they would prepare this night, and what items they would find a way to pack in the morning.

"Reginald," Nathan asked, "How are you going to

open the cans? And how are we going to cook the food? We don't have a can opener *or* a stove!"

Nathan's voice held despair and Reginald once again ruffled his hair before pulling out his trusty swiss army knife.

"Did I mention I was a Boy Scout in my early years?" he asked with a wink. Using his swiss army knife, he showed Nathan how to open the cans, and then how to start the fire. Nathan was enthralled.

"Here, son," Reginald said, holding out the tool in the palm of his hand. "My daddy handed down this tool to me when I became a Boy Scout, and I never had a boy. Now that you are a Boy Scout, I think you should have it."

Nathan beamed with pride as he curled his fingers around it.

"Thanks, Mr. Reginald!" He whooped. "Do you see, Jenny? I'm a Boy Scout now!"

His chest puffed up with pride, not even knowing what a boy-scout was, and Jenny stifled a giggle.

"That's great." She said, carefully removing their pilfered cans from the fire. "Dinner is just about done. It just needs to cool for a minute."

Once the food was cooled, they ate with their hands as no utensils could be found and their stomachs quite content, they settled around the fire, occasionally throwing on more debris as it was getting cooler by the minute. Soon, Nathan curled up against Jenny. The kitten, stuffed on a can of tuna followed suit and Reginald and Jenny quietly whispered, discussing the day's events, and their hopes and fears for the future.

"You know what disturbs me?" Jenny asked. "Besides you, we haven't seen another living soul in hours. Not even the dead, not that I would like to see that again." She shuddered at the thought of poor Miranda and Ron.

"I was thinking the same thing," Reginald replied thoughtfully. "Maybe we are just seeing what we want to see... the thriving." He shrugged. "Anyway, I have seen enough for this day. I think I will rest my eyes now and hope that tomorrow is a brighter day."

Jenny wished him good night, closed her eyes and fervently hoped for the same thing before sleep took her into a sweet, dreamless oblivion.

Chapter 6

The rest of the walk to the police station was slow and relatively uneventful, considering. As they neared the building, more and more people were spotted walking in the same direction, as if the idea were a unified one. It was a very welcome sight, and each person looked as bedraggled and dirty as Jenny felt. She had never wished for a shower more.

Reginald chattered along the way and Jenny learned quite a few things about the interesting man. He was a widower; he had informed them. He had married his high school sweetheart and they had shared 50 years together before cancer had taken her away. Together, they had a daughter, but had lost her to an accidental drowning when she was just a toddler. They never had any other children after burying her. It seemed to Jenny that Reginald had seen more than his fair share of loss in his life.

"Jenny," Nathan called, the kitten still clutched possessively in his arms. "The police station is still here!"

"I can see that." Jenny replied.

She felt relieved at the sight of the brick building with its uniformed officers standing around, directing the stragglers here and there. The tension she had not realized she had been carrying eased.

This part of the city appeared to be untouched, and a gathering was beginning to form with all the people that had survived the event. The grass was still green, the trees upright, birds chirped happily on perches, it was a sight for sore eyes to the weary travelers.

A tent had been put up for shade and served as a mess hall of sorts where water bottles and energy bars were being passed out. Blankets had been placed of the ground and people sat on them in groups, striking up conversation with others in a low hum.

As they neared, a uniformed officer approached them, intent on directing them to their designated areas. He was tall and muscular, his uniformed shirt tight across his chest and arms. The man was an attractive male, as were most in uniform, Jenny considered before mentally slapping herself. This was not the time to be noticing such things.

"Are any in your party in need of medical attention?" he asked in a low baritone. As they all shook their heads in denial, he continued his practiced speech.

"If you would like to head over to the tent, water and a snack will be provided. There is limited space inside, so we are asking that the young remain outside and the elderly report inside. A cot will be provided for you, Sir." The officer said pointedly to Reginald. He then turned and walked away, moving on to direct the next group.

The trio, plus one kitten headed over to the tent, gratefully retrieved their water and snacks and then said their goodbyes to each other.

"It sure was a pleasure meeting you, Miss Jenny, Mister Nathan." Reginald called over his shoulder with a few nods as he entered the police station.

Jenny and Nathan waved and then found an empty spot on one of the blankets beside a lamppost and sat with their backs to the concrete encasing it.

Lucky curled herself into a ball in Nathan's lap and then dexterously turned herself so that she was belly up. Her paws batted playfully at Nathan's little fingers. Jenny and Nathan both grinned at each other, the distraction more than welcome. They watched in amusement as the kitten grabbed hold of Nathan's hand, drawing it nearer to her mouth, mock biting it. The kitten was very delicate despite the play act.

"Does that hurt?" A little girl asked as she sat down in front of Nathan, her mother soon following.

She reached a hand toward the kitten then retracted it, obviously curious and slightly afraid.

"No." Nathan replied without looking up from his prized possession. "Lucky is a sweet kitty."

"Oh." The girl responded gaily. "Can I play with your kitty too?" she asked sweetly.

Nathan shrugged, not really wanting to share his new kitten, but also remembering his manners about sharing.

The two children played with Lucky, alternately giggling and laughing over its antics. Jenny and the girl's mother, that fact being confirmed, began small talk, pointedly avoiding the topic of the tornado. It spoke to an assumed wish for normalcy.

During a lull in their somewhat forced conversation, Jenny took a moment to look around them and felt a sense of pride in her community. During this tragedy, the community pulled together and the kindnesses that she saw reminded her of the gift of human kindness and endurance.

More and more people converged, and the sounds rose to higher levels. The voices were not that of despair, despite the tragedy that had befallen them. The people looked to one another with tender-eyed appreciation as they shared their possessions and a kind word. It did not matter that they were all caked with dirt, some with streaks of blood from various wounds. They acted as though their condition was an everyday appearance. It truly was a sight to see, and it filled Jenny's heart with warmth.

"Everything comes in threes!!!!" A voice suddenly yelled from somewhere amid the crowd. "Everything comes in threes!!!"

The crowd hushed and parted, making way for a young woman, yelling at the top of her lungs. The people surrounding her cowered away as if her words were an unwelcome disease, one that they had no wish to contract.

Jenny was able to catch a glimpse of the woman a moment before law enforcement surrounded her and herded her away from the crowd. The woman had stood on the highest perch of the grassy knoll before the police station, clumps of her own hair tangled between her fingers as she yanked away uncontrollably. Spittle flew from her mouth as she repeated her prophecy like a broken record.

Her words shook Jenny to her core, and her heart slammed in her chest despite her recognition that there was something seriously wrong with that individual. Jenny looked to Nathan and saw that his eyes had widened in fear; of the woman or her words, she had no clue.

"Sissy?" He called out in panic, dragging the startled kitten along as he crawled into her lap. "Sissy… why is that lady screaming?"

Jenny put a comforting arm around him and gave the kitten a soothing pet.

"It's ok, Nathan. She has a sickness in her brain. She doesn't know what she is saying." she offered up the most obvious explanation.

"She's scary." he whispered back.

"I know, Booger. Just ignore her." Attempting to

distract him from the distraught woman being carted away, she drew attention to the kitten still lying in his lap.

"Do you suppose Lucky is hungry? Maybe we should see if it wants some of my granola bar. I'm not really hungry." She said.

Jenny handed Nathan her granola bar and after breaking off small pieces, he offered it to the kitten who sniffed it curiously before snatching it from his fingers greedily. Nathan grunted in approval, the crazy woman forgotten, while he broke off some more small chunks.

Around them, the others seemed to settle, the chatter resumed, and the air of calm returned. It was as though they had unanimously decided to disregard the woman's warnings. A feeling of unease still lingered in the back of Jenny's mind, although she couldn't imagine why. The woman was clearly off her rocker!

Sighing over the absurdity of her feelings, Jenny turned back to converse with the mother before her but was instantly distracted. Out of the corner of her eye, she spotted a mass of birds flying off in a hurry. The ones nearest to her joined the throng. It was a curious sight and the fear at the back of her head niggled in warning.

Once again, all voices hushed as they watched in dismay as the birds took flight. The sky filled with what looked like millions of birds flying harmoniously. The sky was hardly visible from the cloud of flapping wings. Cries and screeches from the various breeds were ominous. The air suddenly felt charged. Something was wrong; something was coming. Red flags waved furiously to those that heeded the warning. Jenny was one of them.

Chapter 7

"Everything comes in threes" replayed like a broken record in Jenny's mind as she watched the sky, that fear scratching feverishly at the back of her head. She rubbed at her head as she looked for signs of another tornado; but the wind was calm, and what bits of sky were visible between the bird's wings was clear. She couldn't place her finger on it but felt deep inside that something was off. Instinctively, she pulled Nathan closer to her.

It started with pebbles. Slowly, so very slowly, they rose from the ground, not quite hovering, but rising higher and higher, inch by inch. Jenny plucked one from the air and stared at it in fascination. It was as though an invisible force held them by a string and was pulling them toward the unknown. The gesture was repeated all around as people plucked pebbles from the air, staring at them in confusion.

Next was hair and clothing, beginning to float upward as if an unseen air blew from beneath them, catching them, and gently lifting them. It seemed harmless enough, merely a prank, until it wasn't.

Larger items began to rise, and the confusion heightened. Jenny stared at a squirrel drifting in mid-air, its body twisting in all directions as it fought the invisible pull. Arms and legs thrashed in the air as it struggled to regain some semblance of balance. Tiny shrieks of panic accompanied its awkward ballet.

"What the..." Someone nearby uttered, the voice echoing Jenny's thoughts. *Hell,* she finished in her head. What the hell summed it up quite succinctly. Higher and higher the squirrel floated until it was out of sight. Jenny blinked a few times, hardly trusting her own eyes. This could *not* be happening!

"Umm, Jenny.." Nathan began from beneath her protective arm.

She shifted her gaze to match his and watched as another squirrel took to the air.

"Why are they flying away?" he asked.

Her mind struggled for an answer, but none came. She had never seen anything like this before. Her only response was a shake of her head.

Soon, larger and larger objects took to the sky. Still in awe, the people around her did not react or panic. But Jenny started to. That niggling in her brain became more insistent and she grabbed on to the lamppost and her arm drew Nathan closer still. Surprised by the action, he released the kitten and then began to protest as he struggled to reobtain the kitten that had started to drift from his arms.

Lucky clawed helplessly at the air, reaching for the safety of Nathan's arms. The kitten's claws dug into the skin of his outreached hand, and he cried out in pain, withdrawing his wounded hand in surprise before he again reached out for it.

"Jenny!" He hollered in a full-on panic.

She too reached for the kitten, momentarily releasing her hold on the lamppost. Realizing she had just let go of their anchor, she pulled her hand back, again wrapping an arm around the lamppost. They both watched helplessly as the kitten, now a feisty ball of fury floated away and out of sight.

An invisible, albeit gentle force began to tug at their bodies, urging them upward, but Nathan did not notice. He beat at his sister's chest in despair.

"You could have caught Lucky, Jenny! Now it's *gone!*" he yelled.

Jenny ignored his outburst and held on tighter to him and the pole grounding them as the pull increased. He angrily protested the protection of her arm, but she would not relent.

Helplessly, she looked around as one-by-one people began to acknowledge the calamity that they were in. She looked into the eyes of the mother she had just been conversing with and noted the fear-stricken look in her eyes as she clutched her daughter to her chest and reached out desperately for help. But Jenny couldn't help; not without endangering herself and her brother.

Voices called out in desperation as they pawed at the air powerlessly. Much like the squirrels they had just admired, their pleas were just as ignored. Those lucky enough to have found an anchor were just as unwilling to give it up as Jenny. Away, the others floated, very, very slowly.

A sort of recognition dawned on Nathan and Jenny felt his body stiffen.

"Jenny? Wha…" he started to speak, but was shocked to silence, his question dying on his lips.

"I know, Nathan. Hold on to me and close your eyes. It will be over soon." she responded, the lie slipping easily from her lips.

In truth, she wondered for the second time if these were their last moments. Fear of the unknown had her in a relentless grip with no end in sight.

Unable to watch for another second, Jenny gripped the lamppost as tightly as she could and squeezed her eyes shut. She could not watch the others flailing and floating away. The idea of it was too horrifying and she felt like her mind would break at any moment; a rubber band stretched too far. Or had it already, and she had been blissfully unaware? She felt much like the crazy woman that had been led away.

As long as she could feel the warm metal in her arms, she knew they were safe. But for how long? How long would this madness continue? The panicked screams tore at her heart, and she longed more than anything to be able to cover her ears, to drown it all out. But that meant letting go of their anchor, and that was something she would not do. Her determination had never been so resolute. They *would* survive this!

"Hang on, Nathan!" she yelled, although her volume seemed unnecessary as the screams were dying out slowly.

He clung to her like a second skin, his arms wrapped so tightly around her it was almost painful.

She felt her arm shift, a fraction of an inch as the pull increased again and for a moment, she was back in the tree with him as the tornado roared its monstrous path. Was this merely a day ago? It felt like days, and yet achingly familiar. Another fraction of an inch and she felt her grip weakening. She did not know how much longer she could hold on.

A rush of emotions slammed through Jenny; fear, defeat, failure, hopelessness and some that were unidentifiable. She was strained to the max in both body and mind. Complete exhaustion threatened to overwhelm her and for a moment, she considered just letting go. Had it been just her, she might have.

New resolve washed over her as she fought to protect her brother; one last tightening of her arm, but it wasn't enough. She no longer had the strength to continue her death-grip on the lamppost, and her arm gave out.

Her eyes met Nathan's, terror echoing in both as a weightlessness came over them. Under any other circumstances, the feeling would have been welcome; exhilarating even. This was not one of those times.

Chapter 8

Jenny and Nathan looked at the ground. Better to watch there, than the vast emptiness above them. Realistically, they were not far from the ground. Had there been any sense of gravitational pull, they could have stood up and been fine. If any comfort could be gained in this moment, that would have been it.

Nathan was cradled to Jenny's chest, and in what she thought were their last moments, she felt an overwhelming love for the little boy. At least, they would die together. That is what she thought anyway, as the ground inched a little further away.

When they had reached about ten feet from the ground, they felt a shift of sorts. Suddenly, as they had been floating upwards, it reversed, and a slow climb downwards ensued. Relief and a bit of hysteria overcame Jenny. She let out a hysterical laugh, completely amazed by their luck. Twice in two days, the pair had dodged a bullet, it seemed.

"Almost there." Jenny whispered, her own voice startling her amongst the eerie quiet.

Her free arm reached for the safety of the ground. She was unable to make contact yet, but they were noticeably closer.

"Nathan, we are almost there." she repeated.

Jenny looked into Nathan's eyes, and where there was profound joy and relief in hers, his eyes were worryingly devoid of emotion. He gave the appearance of an empty shell, completely dead inside. It was as if the traumas of the days had ripped away the light and life from the boy.

"Nathan?" she asked gently, hoping a soothing tone would renew some life in him. "Honey, are you alright? We are almost there. It's going to be okay."

He did not respond, his only response a blank stare.

The ground was finally within reach, and Jenny sank her fingers greedily into the soft grass. Gently, they eased back down like a mother lovingly lying her child down to rest. Never in her life had Jenny appreciated the smell or the feel of grass and dirt so much, or gravity for that matter.

They rested for a moment on the grass, Jenny, at least, appreciative beyond belief. Unsure if the return of gravity would be permanent, however, she quickly scrambled to her feet. Nathan was still held in her arms as she turned toward the police station and ran.

She did not look around to see if anybody else had

survived and was following. Nor did she care about the dictate of the young staying outside. Nothing was going to stop her from entering that building, and nothing would prevent her from staying there. As far as she was concerned, they could stay in that building for the rest of their lives.

Reaching the entrance, she grabbed the handle and flung the door open. A blast of cool and inviting air splashed over them. The refreshing feeling caused goosebumps to form on her arms. The door swung closed, only to reopen a second later as more people flooded inside.

The officer that Jenny had found attractive hurried forward, intent upon halting the group.

"Hey, you guys can't be in here!" he hollered.

"Are you crazy!?" Jenny hollered back, shifting Nathan to her hip. "Did you just see what *happened* outside?"

"Everything floated away! *People* floated away!" A voice called out angrily from behind her.

The officer scoffed in obvious disbelief. It was apparent the inhabitants of the building had not been witnesses to the unbelievable event or had been affected.

"Things don't just float away." He replied tersely. "Now, you people need to go back outside. We don't have the capacity for any more people in here."

"Well, you had better make room." Jenny championed for the small and vastly diminished group forming behind her. "Because we are *not* leaving! I don't know what is happening out there, but *nobody* is safe out there!"

With that said, she and the others rushed forward and around the now red-faced officer.

"Well hold on now!" he blubbered, but nobody was listening and with a shrug, he gave up.

Moving further into the building, Jenny spotted Reginald sitting on a bench by a wall, and grateful to see a familiar face and she hurried over to him. He and the others already comfortable in their sanctuary looked at the crowd in obvious confusion.

"What is going on?" he asked as she neared him.

"I don't even know." she replied. "We were outside, and everything started floating. I don't know how that can happen. But it did. Everything just floated away; people, squirrels, everything. I feel like I'm losing my mind. Or this is one twisted nightmare."

Reginald nodded his head a few times in understanding, and irritation struck Jenny. How could he readily accept her story when she could hardly believe it herself? Recognizing it would be unfair to unleash her irritation on the kind man, she took a few deep breaths to calm herself. It was certainly not his fault that her mind was snapping.

"Nothing like that happened in here?" Jenny asked, even though the answer was obvious.

Reginald shook his head in denial. "Nothing out of the ordinary in here, Miss Jenny."

Reginald patted next to him on the cot that he was resting on, and Jenny and Nathan both sat.

Looking at Nathan, Jenny was concerned. In a matter of minutes, he had gone from a sweet, mischievous child, to one of complete sullen silence. More disturbing was the fact that he had not shed a tear after his tirade. Some form of emotion would have been a relief to Jenny, but he seemed devoid. He had survived the tornado but watching the kitten float away appeared to be his breaking point. Jenny only hoped he would recover in time.

"Mister Nathan, where is the ki…" He broke off at the shake of Jenny's head. He seemed to instinctively understand that it was a volatile topic and politely dropped the matter.

Conversation halted, as neither adult knew what to say now, and the child was silent as a tomb. Jenny looked around the room and studied the faces around her. On them she saw mixtures of fear, confusion, pain and resignation. It was disheartening after the community atmosphere they had all experienced just a short time ago.

The officer walked by, speaking into his radio, his face perplexed and a little bit angry.

"Officer Thompson to Officer Ramsey… are you reading me?" Silence was his answer, and he swore under his breath. "Where the hell *is* she?"

Jenny closed her eyes, fearing she knew the answer to that. Well, part of the answer anyway. What boggled Jenny's mind was where did they all *go*? If the rest of them had descended, then why hadn't they all? Suddenly, her head throbbed in pain. Whether it was from thinking too hard, or the blow to the head she had suffered the previous day, she couldn't say, but she needed an aspirin.

Officer Thompson walked quickly to a door in the back, regaining Jenny's attention and she stared curiously as he furiously ripped a door open and closed it just as hard behind him as he entered.

"He seems a mite angry," Reginald remarked, and Jenny nodded in agreement. "I suppose I would be too if I suddenly found myself responsible for the welfare of this little crowd." He nodded toward the group of survivors claiming a good fraction of the police station.

A few minutes later, Officer Thompson returned and as he stood in the doorway, looking completely overwhelmed, a familiar voice could be heard shouting once again. A chill went up Jenny's spine, and Nathan instinctively drew closer to her side.

"Everything comes in threeeeeeees!!" The voice shouted, louder and louder, and Officer Thompson turned back toward the room. Murmurs filled the main room, growing louder and louder by the minute.

"Hush now! You are scaring everybody! Just be quiet

for a minute would you!" he yelled back impatiently. But the voice kept yelling her message over and over.

The sound caused the itching in Jenny's scalp to resume, and she scratched at it furiously, to no avail. The itch would not go away, and she couldn't help but wonder if it was a premonition of sorts and perhaps the crazy lady wasn't as crazy as she seemed.

Officer Thompson, his face furiously red, and drawing the club from his side, re-entered the room housing the crazed woman. A hush fell over the main room as they all listened intently. The woman's screams were muted through the now closed door, until they were no more. Silence emanated from that room, and a minute later, Officer Thompson returned, looking oddly relieved.

Chapter 9

"Did you kill her?" Someone demanded from across the main room. And a chorus of voices echoed her dismay.

Officer Thompson shook his head emphatically.

"No, I just helped her sleep for a bit is all! She wouldn't stop her ranting and it was creeping me out!" He tried to defend himself to no avail.

The group looked at him angrily, eyes flashing from all around the room, and he adjusted his collar as he debated on where he could hide to avoid their ire. Pulling keys from his side, he ducked into another back area, the lock clicking behind him as he shut himself in. For a moment, Jenny had to wonder how she had ever found the man attractive. His cowardice showed what his figure had not, one of the ugliest individuals she had ever seen.

"Well now," Reginald said, "That man was about as useless as tits on a bull. Pardon my language, Miss Jenny,"

"He probably did us all a favor running and hiding

like that. I sure hope that poor little lady is going to be alright." he continued.

"I will go and check on her," Jenny said, rising to her feet. She couldn't say why exactly, but she felt drawn to the woman and the need to see her was overwhelming.

"I will try to talk to him," Reginald whispered quietly, nodding toward the still silent Nathan, and Jenny nodded back, her appreciation apparent in her eyes.

Nathan stayed behind on the cot, looking off into nowhere as Reginald quietly whispered in his ear. Jenny frowned, her worry, but walked to the door leading to the crazed woman. Pushing gently, she was surprised when the door swung open easily, and she realized that in his haste, Officer Thompson had forgotten to lock the door. *Inept idiot,* she thought to herself.

Slipping inside, Jenny discovered two rows of unoccupied cells lining each wall. She was briefly aggravated recalling the precinct's "no room" mandate before she heard a groan from a cell tucked far in the back. Granted, there weren't a lot of cells, but surely some of the others would have fit inside.

Drawing closer to another groan, Jenny peered through unclosed bars in the furthest cell to finally see up-close the woman behind the rantings. Taken aback, she was surprised to find the woman looking rather angelic in her unconscious state.

Her face was one of the most beautiful that Jenny had

ever seen. The woman had china-doll-pale skin, a tiny button nose, small and rosy puckered lips and long eye lashes that most women would kill for. Jenny guessed her to be close to her own age, whereas during her rants, she appeared much older.

Slightly marring, but certainly not detracting from her beauty was the missing patches of long mahogany brown hair that she had recently torn from her own head, evidenced by dried, patchy scabs. Also adorning her head was a wound to the top of her skull which was bled freely, quite obviously caused by Officer Dickhead when he "put her to sleep."

Jenny hurried into the cell and looked around for something to staunch the flow of blood. After quickly scanning the tight quarters, she discovered it was surprisingly bare. Other than the cot that the woman "slept" on, there was not another item in there. Not even a blanket or pillow for comfort. Briefly, she felt a twinge of pity for any soul that had been previously locked in here. An animal was treated better.

Finding nothing of use and noting that the blood was not stopping on its own, she hesitated for a moment out of embarrassment and then removed her own shirt. Careful to turn it inside out so that the cleanest parts (if you could call it that) were exposed, she gently pressed it to the oozing blood and then slowly applied more pressure.

Jenny pulled the shirt back every few minutes and was

pleased to see that the blood flow was slowing, and she was able to look at the wound itself. She was relieved that it did not appear deep in appearance, but she did not envy the headache the woman would wake up to.

"Thank you." A whispered voice floated up to her, shocking in its calmness.

Since her first sight of the woman, she had only heard her screaming and ranting. To hear her so quiet and serene was startling.

Jenny looked down into the bluest, crystalline eyes she had ever seen.

"You're we-we-welcome." She stammered, appalled by her sudden lack of words and apparent intelligence. "It has almost stopped bleeding. Does your head hurt much? I can see if I can find some aspirin for you."

"No. I will be fine. But again, thank you for your kindness."

Jenny nodded, still unsure what to say. She dabbed awkwardly at the wound, even though it had finally clotted and ceased its spewing.

"I wasn't always crazy," the woman's lyrical voice spoke again, slightly morose this time. "When I was younger, I used to be a psychic. I could see things before they happened. Good things, bad things, it was a blessing and a curse."

"What happened?" Jenny asked curiously.

"Medication," she replied with scorn lacing her angelic

voice. "My parents were bible-thumping catholics and didn't believe in premonitions. They felt they were visions of the devil, so they had me medicated. Schizophrenia was the official diagnosis. It comes and goes now that I've been off the medication for a while."

"Why are you telling me this?" Jenny asked in confusion.

"Because I have seen your purpose and I need you to know that I am not crazy so you can fulfill it. For most of us, this is it. We are 'at the end,' but not you. You will be instrumental to our continuation." A chill ran up and down Jenny's spine at the foreboding words.

"How long have you been off your meds?" she asked, trying her best to be diplomatic and not demonstrate her panic and dismay at the woman's speech.

"Long enough to see clearly again." Was her only reply before the woman shut her eyes again, her face a mask of obvious pain.

"I will get you that aspirin." Jenny replied, while adorning her bloody shirt and fervently avoiding the topic at hand. "You look like you could use it."

A voice in her head wondered if the spoken words were truly that of premonition or lack of medication. Something deep inside told her it was the first, and a shiver coursed her suddenly cool body.

Chapter 10

Walking back into the main room, Jenny felt numerous eyes upon her. The area was quiet and pensive. She could only imagine how she appeared, returning in a blood-stained shirt. Blood that was obviously not belonging to her. The attention made her skin crawl, but she "put on her big girl panties," and took the opportunity handed to her by their attentiveness.

"She is alright," She shyly announced to the group. "But she was struck in the head and could really use some aspirin if anybody has some that they would be willing to share. I have managed to stop the bleeding and it doesn't look deep, but she is obviously hurting."

A few women rushed forward, purses in hand, a luxury Jenny missed already, having left hers behind yesterday morning in lieu of a wallet. More aspirin was shoved into her hands than a pharmacy could provide, and the questions and angry statements followed.

It was quickly apparent that Officer Jerk-face was

definitely better off in his hiding spot, or he might at that moment receive equal, if not more of the same punishment. The woman had seemed crazed, and nobody had liked her message, but not a soul in this building, save him, had wanted to see harm come to her. There had been too much of that already in the last 24 hours.

A petite, but stout woman latched onto Jenny's arm, gaining her full attention.

"What does the poor dear need besides the aspirin?" The woman asked, and Jenny could almost *see* all the ears around her perk up, ready to assist in any way they could.

"Well, she could definitely use a pillow and a blanket. The cell they put her in is open, but it doesn't have anything in it but the cot she is laying on." Jenny replied, and the quickly growing, yet small crowd, drew closer, murmuring their disappointment in the system to each other.

Within moments, a blanket, pillow, more aspirin, several bottles of water, a few granola bars, hygiene products and who knows what was shoved into her arms, all for the woman in the cell beyond the door. It was heartening, and heavy.

"Let me help you with some of that," Reginald spoke from her side, his voice a balm to her frazzled nerves.

Jenny had never felt comfortable with crowds. He eased some of her burden, and when Nathan appeared, still silent, at his side, the burden was eased a bit more.

Several of the curious women offered their assistance,

in obvious jealousy, and not wanting to miss out on the spectacle. It was decided, however, that they would take shifts keeping an eye on their newfound patient, so they did not overwhelm the woman with too much attention at once.

Taking the first "shift," the trio returned to the woman's cell with their gifts. They found the woman sitting on her cot, her hand covering her wound, a pained expression on her face. Reginald quietly handed her some aspirin and water bottle, and after she had downed both, quickly introduced them, polite as ever.

"Ma'am, I am Reginald," he stated, "And these are my new friends, Jenny, and her little brother, Nathan. I'm so pleased to meet you, and I hope you are feeling better soon."

The woman nodded her thanks and introduced herself as Maddie, a name that somehow suited her angelic appearance.

"I'm pleased to meet you all, and I thank you for getting these things for me." She gestured to her donated belongings.

Nathan shifted uncomfortably from leg to leg before moving to a corner of the cell and sitting with his back to the bars. Jenny moved to sit next to him, but he scooted away from her, as if abhorrent to her close presence. It stung, but Jenny shifted to give him more space.

Not missing the spectacle, Maddie giggled and turned to Jenny.

"Nevermind that," she said. "He has an important

role as well and you two will be close again. He will lead you both to your future. It will just take a bit of time. His spark will reignite."

"Fascinating!" Reginald crowed encouragingly and clapped his hands in delight as if he had just seen the most marvelous parlor trick. "Can you see the future, Miss Maddie?"

"I can," She stated emphatically. "And that is why they had me medicated."

Reginald tsked and inwardly, Jenny scoffed.

"This one," Maddie stated authoritatively, nodding toward Jenny, "She is meant to be our continuation. And this one," this time nodding toward Nathan, "He is to be the way, the guide as you will."

Reginald bobbed his head several times in agreement, a trait that was beginning to get on Jenny's nerves, before closing his eyes for a moment as if in deep concentration.

"I can see that, Miss Maddie. You might be right."

With a few more annoying head bobs, he sat down next to Maddie, after asking her permission first, of course. Jenny suddenly found the jail cell as stifling as it was meant to be and quickly exited without a word. Nathan following silently on her heels.

"Could you please see if you can find me a television, Jenny?" Maddie asked as she passed the cell bars on her way out. Jenny agreed to see if she could find one and hastily left.

Chapter 11

Re-entering the main room had a completely different feel to it the second time, much to Jenny's relief. Everybody in the room was occupied with idle chit-chat or various activities and paid her no attention, much to her relief.

"C'mon, Nathan, let's have a look around." she said.

He followed her as she rounded the room, investigating closets and cabinets. She was just nearing another cabinet when she felt a hand gently latch on to her arm.

"What are you looking for?" The stout woman asked her.

"Maddie, the woman in the cell, asked for a television. I'm not really sure why, since I doubt very much there will be anything on, but I figured it couldn't hurt to look."

"Oh!" The woman gasped. "I saw a television on a stand in a back room! Larry!" She yelled, causing Jenny to jump. "Larry! Come here and help us roll a television to the poor dear in the back!"

Her assumed partner, Larry hurried over to assist.

Jenny was shocked at the differences between the two. Where the woman was stout, he was a bean pole. Where she appeared intrusive, he was standoffish. If the cliché opposites attract was accurate, here was a demonstration of it right before her.

"Yes dear?" Larry asked quietly and followed dutifully as the woman latched onto his arm and dragged him toward a back room that Jenny had not yet investigated.

Forming the caboose of this odd train, Jenny and Nathan trailed behind the pair. She listened with mirth as the woman explained in detail his assignment and how very important it was to her.

Minutes later, they were rolling an old television on a cart down the cell block, much to Maddie's delight. One long extension cord later and they turned it on to find nothing but static. Nathan settled back into his corner and blankly watched the nothingness that filled the screen.

Maddie flipped a knob, scanning the channels, static after static channel, which came as no surprise to Jenny. Letting out a sigh, Maddie sat back down next to Reginald and gave him a wink.

"It's just not time yet, Reginald." She told him in a matter-of-fact tone. He did his annoying head bob, his faith in her word finite.

"Time for what?" Larry asked curiously, a puzzled look on his face.

"You will see." She replied cryptically.

Larry and his stout wife, Annie, as she was introduced to the cell, settled in next to Maddie and Reginald on the cot, and struck up conversation. The cell was beginning to feel extremely crowded, so Jenny took that as a sign that her "shift" had ended and once again hastily retreated.

This time, Nathan did not follow. In truth, he did not appear to even notice her exit. He sat on the cold floor of the cell staring at the television, not really seeing it. It hurt her heart to see.

Once back in the main room, Jenny searched for a quiet spot where she could sit by herself. After the last twenty-four hours, she had a lot to process, and it was quickly catching up with her now that everything was calmer. She found an unoccupied corner of the room and sat heavily on the floor; her body suddenly wearier than it had ever been before.

Jenny leaned her head back to rest on the wall and she closed her eyes. Ignoring the low hum of people talking in the background, she allowed herself to think of the recent events. Her body began to tremble uncontrollably, and in a way, she was relieved to find that she was not as numb as her brother was now.

She had no idea how long she sat against the wall, but her bones felt stiff and achy. Her eyes had grown heavy, and she was sure she had dozed off for at least a few minutes, perhaps longer. Slowly, voices began to trickle into her consciousness, and she caught snatches of words, then full sentences. Enough of the conversation filled her ears to know that she did not want to open her eyes just yet.

"We need to make a supply run." Some brave voice spoke from somewhere nearby. A few voices added their agreement, and silently, Jenny called them fools. No way did *she* want to go back out there. Who knew what would happen next!

"Are you *crazy*?" A voice from across the room echoed Jenny's thoughts. "We don't even know what *that* was! It could happen again, and *then* what? No way am I going out there!"

"We can't stay locked in here forever without supplies!" Yet another voice hollered.

"We will starve without supplies!" A few more voices chimed in their loudly growing agreement. Just as many voices then opposed.

The argument went back and forth until one could be dizzy just from listening. Eventually, it was agreed that a small party of 10 volunteers would head out to the nearest gas station, a mere two blocks away, and return with as many supplies as they could carry.

10 brave souls exited the 19th precinct that day, men and women alike, carrying with them the hopes of those left behind. Hours later, it was woefully apparent to the rest of the group that they weren't coming back.

Jenny was not surprised in the least. There was much speculation as to what had happened to the small party, but the answer was never clear. They appeared to have simply vanished.

Chapter 12

The hours ticked by comfortably, despite the chorus of growling bellies. The granola bars, which had done nothing to sate their appetites, had been passed around fairly and long since been depleted.

The comfortability made Jenny nervous and on edge. It was *too* quiet, and she could not help but wonder if she had found a pessimistic side to herself, or if the foreboding she felt was warranted.

Having had enough time to wallow, Jenny rose from her quiet corner to seek out her brother, hoping for a miracle and that she would find him returned to his old, mischievous self. Returning to the cell where she had last seen him, she found him sitting in the same position as she had left him.

The television he stared at still held static, and little more. Periodically, Maddie or Reginald would rise and change the channel, only to see more of the same. It seemed rather pointless to Jenny.

As if by a long-awaited miracle, the screen changed, and a familiar face appeared. Gretchen Pike, a news anchor of WNBC, was a face easily recognizable. Her stories on current events were feverishly popular, particularly with the male viewers, most probably in part to her exceedingly voluptuous curves.

"This is Gretchen Pike," she stated the obvious, flipping her long, blonde hair in her signature move. "All around the world, for the last twenty-four hours, tornados have sprouted up in what experts now call an unlikely and unforeseen event. Meteorologists have been working around the clock to figure out why these events are happening and attempting to find a more efficient way to predict them. As of right now, they do not have any answers, and their official standing is 'No comment.' Please, stay with us live as we anxiously await their expertise and guidance."

"Ugh," Annie grunted under her breathe. "I can't stand her."

"Why? She's great!" Larry responded, perplexed by his wife's attitude.

Annie shrugged her shoulders and let out an undignified snort. "You would. Every man loves her."

Commercials commenced and Jenny ignored them, turning her attention to Nathan instead, who was now watching the television intently. She was pleased to see that some life had returned to him and let out a silent sigh of relief. Gone was the blank stare, and Jenny fervently hoped that it never returned. It had been eerie to see someone so full of life become so numb.

Ending mid-commercial, Gretchen's face reappeared on the screen, excitement evident on her face. She was practically bouncing in her seat.

"For those of you just tuning in, I am Gretchen Pike with WNBC, covering the recent tornados that have been popping up across the world. This just in is video footage of a new world-wide anomaly. It appears as if for a period of about 10 minutes earlier today there was an unexplained 'gravity shift' of some sort. WNBC has been in contact with NASA and NOAA for some kind of explanation, but there appears to be none at this time. A survivor of this anomaly has sent us video footage which has been verified as legitimate as it is back by several others across the globe. I am told to warn viewers that the images are graphic and viewer discretion is advised."

Hearing this, Jenny turned away from the screen, not wishing to see the same horrifying sight twice in one day. Living through it was traumatic enough. Fearing the news footage would set Nathan's recent recovery back, she quickly moved to stand in front of him, trying to block his view. He leaned to the side to look around her, his eyes intent on the screen.

"At this time," Gretchen continued, "there is no explanation for the event or any idea of what happened to the people and animals filmed in this video. NASA and NOAA are working together to find answers, but again the official standing is currently 'no comment.' For other news, I turn it over to my fellow anchorman, Rob Griever. Rob?"

Rob took over, droning on with news that not a soul in the cell cared to listen to and his voice became white noise in the background. Seeming to recover from her shock of validation, Annie jumped up from the cot and without a word darted back to the main room. Larry looked toward her quickly retreating in confusion.

"Where is she going?" He asked to no one in particular.

"I reckon we will find out shortly." Reginald replied.

A few minutes later, the cell became even more crowded as people followed Annie back to the cell, and they sat where they could on the floor, all eyes intently watching the television for more news.

Jenny was suddenly feeling quite claustrophobic. The exit to the cell was blocked by numerous bodies, the number growing by the minute, and she squeezed herself into a corner, making herself as small as possible.

Sweat began to pool between Jenny's breasts and under her arms as a stifling feeling came over her. As more and more people crammed into the tiny cell, Jenny felt the need to escape and quickly rose to her feet, intent on just that. Stepping over limbs, and tripping on some, she almost made it to the exit when she heard Maddie call her name.

"Jenny, you don't want to leave just yet. It's about to happen, and you need to know what you are up against."

A few bystanders turned to look at Maddie, then to Jenny, confusion clear on their faces. The rest kept their eyes glued to the television, much like Nathan, as if possessed by some strange need to know what tragedy would strike next. Jenny shuddered at the thought but halted her retreat.

"Maddie," Jenny started as politely as possible, which was difficult considering her unease. "I know you think you can see the future, and that I hold some big part of it. But it just isn't true. I need some air."

Turning to Nathan, she asked, "Do you want to come with me?" He shook his head, still not speaking to her, his gaze returning to the television.

Jenny nearly made it to freedom when the news returned from its latest set of commercials, and within seconds of its return, she froze mid-stride. Fear, horror and some unnamable emotion laced Gretchen's voice as she rushed out her latest report.

"This is.. oh fuck it." she rushed out, "We just received videos from multiple areas around the globe and although experts haven't legitimized them yet, they appear to be legit. Alien machines have been appearing around the globe, and where they show up, people are disappearing quickly. We will show the footage and then we are going off air to be with our families. Good luck to you all and God bless."

Jenny stared in horror as images of massive machines appeared on screen, bright flashes coming from them in the direction of people that ceased to exist the moment the flash reached them. The screen went dark and static resumed. For a moment, nobody reacted, and then chaos ensued.

Screams erupted from around the cell, and the vast majority of the people crammed into the cell rushed from it, tripping over one another in their haste to get to a window. The scene was eerily familiar and reminded Jenny of the tornado from just yesterday.

Remaining in the cell, which was probably the safest place at that moment was Jenny, Nathan, Maddie and Reginald. Jenny, Nathan and Reginald wore the same shocked look on their faces, while Maddie's was one of affirmation and glee.

"Didn't I tell you? It is just as I saw. Yesterday was the beginning of the end. But you will be the continuation, Jenny. Everything comes in threes." she stated somewhat smugly.

Screams erupted from the main room, the sounds echoing down into the cells. Jenny's breath caught and her heart hammered in her chest at the sound. She didn't have to see to know what those screams meant. She turned to look at Maddie, a wild look in her eyes, but Maddie just grinned and patted her hand.

"Not yet. But when I tell you to go, you *go*." Maddie said in a calming voice that did little to still the pounding in Jenny's chest.

She felt Nathan slip his hand into hers and she attempted to steel herself. If not for her, then for him. He would need her strength, even if it was forced.

"Aren't you two coming with us?" Jenny asked Reginald and Maddie who sat calmly, side by side on the cot. Reginald and Maddie both shook their heads.

"Neither one of us would make it." Maddie said. "We weren't meant to. I am honored to have met two of you."

The ominous good-bye terrified Jenny, but she hid it well. Inside, she did not want to believe Maddie's prophecy. It sounded ludicrous that she and Nathan were meant to survive, while so many others perished.

The niggling itch of foreboding returned to Jenny's brain with a fury. She reached up unconsciously to scratch at her scalp, but it gave her no relief. She could feel deep inside that something major was about to happen, that their lives were irrevocably changed. It unsettled her.

"That feeling that you have inside right now," Maddie warned, "Listen to it. Don't ever ignore it and it will keep you safe. I had a feeling you were a kindred spirit. Now I know."

She paused for a moment, a smile on her angelic face. "It is time. Now *GO!*"

Chapter 13

Scooping Nathan up into her arms, Jenny raced out of the police station. She had no clear direction in mind. Pure instinct and adrenaline were her map. She ran until her lungs screamed in pain and her breaths came out in short gasps.

A stitch in Jenny's side forced her to halt, and finally glancing to see where they were, she was elated to find them in front of a store that held the promise of every supply they could possibly need for this new adventure. She only hoped that it had not already been raided.

Glancing around to be sure no danger lurked around them, and finding none, she walked to the entrance, setting Nathan down beside her. As she approached the double doors, she was surprised to see the doors swing open electronically as if ready for business.

Upon entering, the store looked pristine. There was not a single trace of looting, which came as a surprise. A small twinge of guilt struck Jenny's heart knowing that she was about to do just that. Pushing the feeling aside, she directed her brother toward the backpacks displayed so neatly on their racks.

"Grab a backpack, Nathan." she instructed. "We are going to need them to carry what we need."

Nathan dutifully, but still silently, grabbed a bright blue cookie monster backpack and placed it on his back. Jenny grabbed the largest she could see, which happened to be colored in a black and grey camouflage; perfectly suited to their current needs. Throwing it over one shoulder, she then moved them toward the grocery aisles, grabbing all that she could find that would be hardy and easily opened, and shoving it into her bag.

Her bag was quickly filled and getting uncomfortably heavy by the second, while Nathan's remained devoid of their pilfered items. She refrained from filling his until the last moment, thinking only to fill it with the lightest of items so she did not weigh him down, causing a delay in their escape.

Satisfied that she had adequately supplied them with as much food as necessary at the moment, the pair then turned toward the bedding aisle. Finding two lightweight blankets in rolled perfection, she stuffed them into Nathan's backpack, skipping over the exquisitely comfortable looking pillows that would have never fit.

"I can't think of anything more we could need." Jenny

whispered, the sound carrying through the empty store more like that of a shout.

They made their way to the registers, an ingrained habit, and spotting a three-pack of lighters, she grabbed it and threw that into her pack as well.

Nathan looked at Jenny pointedly, his morals having been solidly ingrained by her parents and then by her, and grudgingly, she pulled a hundred-dollar bill from her wallet and placed it neatly on the register. This might be the end of the world, she thought, but her purchases were probably more than paid for.

The duo headed back to the entrance/exit and Jenny placed herself in front of Nathan. Peering outside, perhaps longer than necessary, she deemed it safe enough, and they escaped as quietly as possible, their ears tuned to every sound.

Again, Jenny had no idea what direction to go in, and she prayed that whatever direction she chose took them as far away from the alien machines as possible. Considering their options, she felt getting them out of the city was probably their best chance.

The where decided, Jenny considered the how. For a moment, she considered checking cars for keys left in them, but quickly tossed the idea away. She had no idea how fast the machines could go, and she was sure that a moving vehicle would make a large, loud target.

Horseback, another ludicrous idea was also not an

option. If there was a horse in Manhattan, she wouldn't have any idea where to find one, or how to ride one at that. Jenny audibly sighed as realization dawned on her. There really was only one option, on foot.

"Nathan," she started, instantly regretting the words she was about to utter. "We need to get out of Manhattan, but we are going to have to do that by walking. It is going to be a long walk and we must do that without making a sound. Can you do that?"

She looked down into Nathan's eyes, which were hardened with a determination she wished she felt. He nodded his head, trusting her judgement, but still not uttering a word. She supposed it was a blessing now, but already she missed the sound of his voice. Bubbly, joyful, full of life and mischief.

They started their trek, keeping as close to buildings as possible to make themselves less visible. Jenny's senses were on high alert. Eyes scanned their surroundings, ears perked for even the slightest sound. Her body was tense with fear and trepidation.

Faster than she expected, they once again found themselves hiking in, over and under wreckage from the tornado. Somehow, the sight was not as appalling to Jenny as it was the first time she had seen it. Too much had happened since then and she was numb to the carnage.

They hiked for long hours without incident until the sun began to retreat from the sky and although she wanted to push on to the safety outside of the city, Jenny knew visibility would soon be a problem. Daylight dimming, her eyes scanned for a place she regarded safe enough to settle down for the night.

The sun had nearly departed the sky when Jenny found a house that was not entirely destroyed. It had shifted and leaned upon the house next to it, and although it looked to be precarious considering typical standards, she supposed it was sturdy enough to hold them for one night at least.

"Come on, Nathan." she whispered, gesturing toward the house. "We will stay here tonight."

He dutifully followed, silent as a mouse.

Chapter 14

The interior of the house came with a fun-house kind of feeling. It was odd to see the floors in place, but the walls crooked. The home-owner's furniture was in obvious disarray. It was certainly not the kind of set-up Jenny would have gone for.

Jenny flipped the couch back up from its overturned position, ignoring the other scattered and upside-down pieces. Nathan immediately flopped onto it, clearly exhausted from their long day. It was easy to forget that he was only four and not as energetic as a full-grown adult when fear was guiding them.

Within minutes, Nathan was asleep and lightly snoring. Taking a blanket from his backpack, she covered him and although exhausted herself, she decided to explore their haven of the night.

Finding the kitchen in better condition than the living room they had entered, she located the stove and testing the knobs, was delighted to see a flame on the outdated range spark to life. The smell coming from the closed fridge told her that it was not in as good condition, and she dared not open it. The cabinets, however, were packed and in perfect condition and she nearly danced with joy. The supplies she had grabbed would last for yet another day since she did not need to use them this night.

Her stomach growled angrily as she took stock of their pilfered supplies and plotted out a meal. After checking the sink to assure they had running water, she located and filled a dented pot with water and began to boil noodles that she had found.

Once done, she added cans of mixed vegetables, canned chicken and cream of mushroom soup all with blessedly made pull tops. While it heated again, she searched for plates and utensils. Locating both, plates were made, and she made her way back to the living room, her mouth salivating from the aroma the entire way.

Jenny regretted waking Nathan, but she was sure he was just as hungry as she was, and she gently shook him until he stirred.

"Nathan," She whispered, "Eat some dinner and then you can go back to sleep."

Nathan opened his eyes, panic clear in his blood-shot eyes, until he realized they were not in any danger, and he grabbed the plate from her hand. He wolfed down his food like he had been starved for days. Jenny did the same. For such a simple meal, it tasted like heaven after only eating granola bars for the entire day.

Their stomachs sated, Jenny set aside their plates and utensils and settled on the couch with Nathan. As was customary for a young boy, Nathan fell back to sleep immediately, nestled securely in her arms. She hugged him close and closed her eyes, feeling imminent sleep upon her as well, but it didn't come.

Exhausted as she was, she was unable to turn off her heightened senses. She lay in the blackest of dark, the most silence she had ever experienced, willing herself to sleep knowing they had another hard day of hiking ahead of them. But sleep would not come. She was jittery in anticipation and dread, the slightest twitch from Nathan's little body causing her to jump.

She remembered advice taken from a sleep app she had once youtubed on a particularly difficult night when her mind would not stop racing. Closing her eyes, she pictured a light oh-so-slowly making its way from her toes and out of her head "forcing all negative energy" out of her limbs. Her limbs loosened upon command, and within minutes, she drifted off into a light sleep.

What could have been minutes or hours later, Jenny was awakened by the loud sound of machinery groaning from movement. The sound steadily moved closer, and she instinctively placed a silencing hand over Nathan's mouth.

"Shhh." Her voice was barely audible as she whispered. "Not a sound, Nathan."

His body stiffened in her arms, and she knew that he was as terrified as she was. She slowly stroked his hair, trying to sooth him, but knew that it was of no use.

The loud sound of mechanical arms and legs drew closer to the house that they hid in, and Jenny rose her head slightly over the couch to peek through the living room window. Nathan tried to pull her back down, his panic visible in his touch, but she easily fought his weak pulls.

The machine halted just outside of the house and a light from the head region appeared to scan the area as it swept back and forth. As the beam of light swept toward their direction, Jenny ducked and tried to shrink their bodies as deep into the couch as possible.

Holding her breath, her body tense and stiff as a board, she listened intently for the machine to move on. She could see the beam of light reflecting on the wall across from them as it swept back and forth before moving on.

Nathan let out a tiny whimper of fear and Jenny quickly, but quietly shushed him. The beam of light returned to the wall, again scanning the room and the machine let out a mechanical whine as it shifted even closer. It was not apparent if the machine had heard their small sounds, but its close proximity worried her.

Nathan curled into Jenny's side, nearly burrowing himself under her. She understood his instinct completely. If there was ever a time for the ground to open up and swallow a person, this was probably that time.

The wait was killing her. Whether they were found, or if they managed a gracious escape, she just wanted something to happen. The limbo they were in was torturous. Adrenaline coursed through her veins and the need to get up and run was nearly overwhelming, but she resisted knowing that was a sure way to a quick death.

In her head, she hummed the lyrics to her favorite song in hopes that it would calm her racing heart. Underneath her, she felt Nathan's racing to the same crazy beat.

What felt like hours, but was probably only mere minutes, they heard the mechanical groans begin again. The stomps of the mechanical legs were almost deafening in the silence as they began to move, away from their location to their joy and relief.

Long after the sounds disappeared and silence once again resumed, the pair lay there, frozen in form until their limbs ached from the strain of their positions.

Nathan was the first to move, and he crawled out from his sanctuary under her and laid on top of her, cuddling himself up to her like an infant to its mother. Large wet tears landed on her chest, falling faster and faster as silent sobs shook his body.

Jenny sat up, pulling him with her and she curled him

into her arms and rocked him. Back and forth, back and forth until finally, his crying stopped, and his breath came in deep shallow breaths. Carefully, she settled him back on the couch and lay beside him.

Chapter 15

Jenny awoke to sunlight streaming through the windows, beaming brightly in her eyes and she was amazed that she had slept at all. She was also appalled that she had slept for so long. She had no idea what time it was, but it was clear that it was far later than she had intended to leave.

Sitting up, she tried to rise without stirring Nathan. He was so exhausted that he only rolled over in his sleep, occupying the spot she had just left. She stretched her sore limbs, groaning quietly at the pain. Her muscles ached like they had never before, and she wondered whether it was the tension of the last couple of days, or if it was the close quarters on their shared couch.

Ignoring that thought, she made her way back to kitchen intent on feeding them one last good meal before they "hit the road" again. She had no idea where they would be staying again tonight, but she hoped that it was out of the city and somewhere safer. She didn't know why, but she was convinced that if they could just make it out of the city, they would have a fighting chance.

Returning to the well-stocked pantry, she looked over her options. Inside, there were more cans of the items she had pilfered the night before. There was also numerous boxes of assorted donuts, puddings, and snack cakes. The homeowners either had several children, or a massive sweet-tooth. Either way, she was grateful.

After careful consideration, she decided to reheat the meal she had made the night before and pack as much of the pantry supplies as she could. Returning to the living room, she scooped up her bag and shoved as much of the supplies in as she could. Taking items out of the boxes helped to save room and she crammed her bag until it was filled to the brim.

Having successfully supplied them, in her opinion, and their meal now warm enough to eat, albeit slightly burnt at this point, she made plates for them both and grudgingly woke Nathan.

This time, Nathan woke screaming and flailing, nearly knocking the plates from her hands. It took a few moments for her to calm him, but realization that they were not in danger sank in and they both settled onto the couch to eat their fare. It did not have the same gourmet taste to it as the night before when they were hungrier than they had ever been, but they ate everything on their plates anyway.

After eating their less than appealing, but necessary meal, they made use of the crooked- non-flushing bathroom, grabbed their bags and exited the house.

The sun was blindingly bright in the clear blue sky, and not a sound could be heard except the gentle tapping of their own shoed feet on the pavement. Not a car drove by, or any birds chirping in a tree. You could easily hear a pin drop it was so quiet. On a normal day, it would have seemed peaceful, tranquil even. But the circumstances behind that silence made it feel oppressive, wrong, and frightening.

Jenny and Nathan walked, hugging buildings as closely as they could, their ears attuned to every sound that they made, and the lack of it otherwise. They were both tense as a strung bow. Just the idea of another sound made them jumpy and ready to flee. It was a very disconcerting feeling waiting for the next nightmare to begin, knowing that it was just there, out of reach.

After miles of walking, Jenny's pack became overbearingly heavy. She shifted the weight from shoulder to shoulder when the pain became too much, but it did not offer much relief. Wishing they had been further along their route before she called a halt to their trek, she quietly urged Nathan into a gas station so that they could take a break.

Nathan immediately headed to the restroom, and Jenny idly looked around as she waited for her turn. Next to the restroom was a map framed on the wall with an arrow pointing to signify "you are here."

Seeing their current location, she was amazed. 20 blocks from her condo to the 19th precinct had taken such a long time to achieve. It had not occurred to her that the present path, which was devoid of the tornado wreckage would be a considerably faster route.

In half a day, the pair had covered that and then some. If the map was accurate, they were nearly to what she considered freedom. The city would be behind them by tomorrow if they continued the pace they were going.

Nathan exited the restroom and flopped onto an overturned crate. Jenny set her bag beside him and urged him to find something in there to eat while she used the facilities herself.

After her necessities, she began to wash her hands out of habit, which quickly became delight. The feel of the cool water on her hands was pure bliss. Almost in desperation, she cupped the cool water and sank her face into her hands. It felt strange to be so delighted over something so simple as running water.

After scrubbing as much surface area as she could manage in a tiny one stall bathroom, she felt almost new, refreshed, and certainly a little better in spirit. She rejoined Nathan, and digging into her bag of goods, pulled out an individually wrapped donut to eat.

After devouring her snack, Jenny looked around

the store, mostly out of curiosity, knowing she couldn't possibly hold any more than she already had in her pack. Nosing through the drawer in the back office, she was surprised to find an old Walkman. Clicking it open, she found a Bob Marley tape inside. She was impressed by the owner's taste.

Nathan, following closely behind, as if she would disappear at any moment, glanced between her and the Walkman curiously. Carefully placing the attached headphones on his ears, and pressing the play button, her heart beat an extra, albeit happy beat, to see a sudden smile on his face. It was the first she had seen in what felt like forever, and it melted her heart to see it return.

The pair sat there for a while, him on the crate, headphones secured in place, and her on the floor, carefully selecting items from her bag of goods until they were stuffed, rested, and ready to continue their adventure. For a brief moment, a feeling of contentment came over them and they savored it, knowing that it would not last. Whatever "this" was that was happening, it wasn't over yet, and they both could feel it.

Rising to her feet, Jenny studied the map on the wall intently when a huge obstacle occurred to her. They might be making incredible progress, but how to cross the Hudson river? There were only a couple of ways across, and none seemed feasible to her.

Her lower lip clenched firmly in her teeth; she literally

chewed the problem over. No immediate answer sprang to mind. The bridges across were, in her opinion, too far of a distance. They would also be completely exposed, should they take that route.

So intent on solving the riddle before her, she did not hear Nathan's approach, alarming, considering their current need for complete attentiveness. His little hand lightly touched her arm, and she nearly jumped out of her skin.

Nathan peered up at her, an unspoken question in his eyes, and internally, she debated whether to share with him the latest debacle they were in. She sighed audibly, causing a fleeting moment of panic to reflect in his eyes.

"We need to get out of Manhattan," She whispered, "But that means we have to cross the Hudson river, and I don't know how we are going to do it without being seen."

A look of understanding crossed his face, quickly over-shadowed by an "ah ha" expression. In the minutes she had stared at the map, considering their options, she had no forthcoming answer. Upon hearing the problem, a solution immediately came to his mind and he was so sure of his idea that he was practically vibrating. It was disconcerting and a little bit ego-deflating.

Without a word, he grabbed her hand, his headphones again securely in place. He dragged her toward the exit, a smile on his face. She didn't know what he had in mind, but an odd feeling told her she was not going to like it.

Chapter 16

The pair hiked in their resumed silence for what felt like an exceedingly long time. Nathan appeared content with his new Walkman; the sound of Bob Marley soothing him, while Jenny was going crazy inside from the strain of attentiveness.

The crunch of their footsteps sounded like a cannon going off in the utter silence surrounding them. The only positive she could find was that they would definitely have an early warning of trouble if the sound of footsteps was so noticeable. Still, this knowledge did nothing to calm her nerves.

Once again, despite their earlier gorging, Jenny's pack was beginning to feel heavier by the minute. The weight was nearly unbearable, and she began to consider whether they actually *needed* all of the supplies that she carried. Determining that yes, the supplies were necessary, she began to think of various ways she could ease the burden without losing the load.

Jenny was so lost in thought that it took her by surprise to realize that they had reached the Hudson river and were approaching a dock adjoined to it. Looking at Nathan, she observed that he was, albeit silently, overjoyed by the sight before them. He beamed and grinned ear to ear.

Docked on both sides were small boats, personally owned vessels by the look of them. Expensive, personally owned boats, she noted to herself, which came as no surprise considering they were in Manhattan.

As they entered the dock, she began to read the names of the vessels, mostly out of curiosity. The first set tied to the dock were "The Mary" on their left, "The Mistress" on their right. The next set were "Lil Fishy" and "Lost the house, won the boat." The final set, near the end of the dock, had Jenny choke back a much-needed laugh. To her left was "Smells fishy," and on the right was "The Pussy Boat."

Jenny let out an audible, indelicate snort of humor before clapping a hand over her face to silence herself. Nathan pulled his headphones down and looked at her questioningly, but she just shook her head at him.

"I will explain when you are older. Much, much older." She whispered to him. Inside, she caught the irony of how she had once dreaded the day that they had "the birds and the bees talk," now she just hoped they lived to see that day.

Nathan shrugged and started toward "Smells fishy."

He had nearly climbed aboard when Jenny stopped him with an arm.

"You know we can't take a boat, right? It would be just as loud as a car." She whispered to him.

Nathan rolled his eyes as if she were stating the obvious and dodged her arm. Climbing aboard, he began to root through its items, intently searching for God-knows-what. Jenny watched from the dock, puzzled, and suddenly apprehensive.

Why she was following the lead of a four-year old was beyond her, but she continued to watch, her curiosity piqued. Again, a feeling of foreboding washed over her as she watched him pick up and discard item after item. Whatever he was searching for was the next step in their crazy adventure. She knew it deep down and dreaded it simultaneously.

Not finding what he was looking for on the first boat, Nathan climbed to the next, and then the next until aboard the "Lil Fishy" he discovered what he was searching out. 2 life vests were thrown in her direction, which she caught by miracle since he couldn't throw, and she couldn't catch: neither being athletic in any way. When he scrambled back onto the dock, it was Jenny's turn to look quizzical.

"I don't understand, Nathan." she started, "If we aren't taking a boat, why do we need the vests?"

Nathan mock slapped his forehead, shook off his backpack and began to put on the life vest. Still unsure of his plan, she hurried to do the same. Life vest secured, he again placed his pack on his back and watched as she did the same.

She eyed him closely, curious what his next step was when he did the unexpected. Without a word, he turned around, ran the length of the dock and leapt into the Hudson river.

She moved as quickly as she could to stop him when his intentions dawned on her, but she was too late. With a splash, he hit the water and began to float downstream, his body bobbing above the water.

Hesitating only the barest of moments, she jumped and gasped in shock at the cool temperature of the water. Her limbs stung for a moment, the water cooler than she had expected, but, recovering, she hurried her movements to catch up to her brother. She latched onto his arm and pulled him close to her so they wouldn't be separated as they floated away at a faster speed than she would have liked.

After a few minutes, having not bathed in a couple of days; or perhaps because of the heat of the past days, the water began to feel refreshing despite its murky appearance.

Bits of debris floated around the pair, which they gently shooed away with their hands. For a moment, Jenny wondered if the debris was remnants of the tornados, or if it was just human pollution, which she emphatically opposed. Either way, it did not matter to her. It was there.

Prior to "the incidents" as she labeled them in her mind, the one and only organization she had dedicatedly donated to was Earth Now. It was an organization devoted to cleaning up their planet and she had personally attended a few of their highway cleaning events.

How naïve she had been. Proudly, she had believed that her little contributions had made a difference. The evidence suggesting otherwise now surrounded her, a nagging, silent voice telling her that her efforts had not been enough.

Pulling her from her thoughts, realization slapped her in the face as the current noticeably picked up. "Safe" in their life-vests, they began to bob up and down at a more furious rate.

Each bob forced them just below the surface and they coughed and sputtered after each dunking. The water tasted rancid as it filled their mouths and they gagged uncontrollably, their stomachs resisting the putrescent invasion.

Instinctively, Jenny stretched her legs, feeling for the bottom to steady them both, but the bottom was out of her reach. Grabbing Nathan around the waist with one arm, she windmilled the other arm trying to swim them to shore. It was awkward, but slowly effective. Her arms and legs burned from the strain, and she felt more than saw Nathan adding his own limbs to her efforts.

The closer they got to land, the calmer the current and they were able to catch their breath. Hugging the shoreline, they floated on their backs, resting their exhausted limbs.

"I don't know about you," Jenny stated quietly, "But I do *not* want to do that again!"

Nathan nodded his agreement and let out a residual gag that turned Jenny's stomach. She did not even want to think about how much of the filthy water they had ingested, or the parasites and bacteria it contained. The idea of it was horrifying.

They floated downstream, occasionally having to swim their way closer to shore when they began to drift back toward the middle of the river. Looking around, Jenny noted that their surroundings were beginning to look less city-like and more rural. She had no idea where they were, but it suddenly dawned on her that in their struggle in the currents, they had actually crossed the Hudson river.

"You clever boy!" She exclaimed excitedly, and he grinned from ear to ear.

The further they floated, the more debris they encountered until the point it was bordering on dangerous. Large trees floated around them, others were wedged in the muck, and they were forced to navigate around them. As the level of debris raised, Jenny decided to look for a good spot to go ashore, deciding their river trip had to end before one or both of them got hurt.

After a few more minutes, Jenny spotted a rather large, wooded area with a shallow shoreline, and she guided them both toward the "beach." Pulling their sodden selves from the river, they collapsed onto the grassy beach.

Chapter 17

After lying on the grass for what felt like hours, regaining their strength and recovering from their vigorous swim, back packs and life vests were shed. They enjoyed the weightlessness for a moment before the itch in Jenny's brain returned.

Mechanically, she looked around for the cause, but found none. Instinct told her that they needed to hide, and quickly. Following her intuitive feeling, she grabbed Nathan by his arm, gestured to his bag and after retrieving her own, led him toward the safety of the trees and brush.

Their bags felt monumentally heavy as they made their way to the treeline, soaked through as they were, but the pair hurried as much as their burdens would allow.

Upon reaching what appeared to be a temporary haven, Jenny wanted to feel relief, but a nagging feeling told her they were not out of the woods just yet. Finding a heavily shrubbed area, she encouraged Nathan into it before following herself, ignoring the sting of pricks from the thorns adorning it.

Jenny and Nathan settled in as comfortably as possible in their thorny haven and heads cocked, they listened to the silence surrounding them in anticipation. Moments later, they were rewarded with the sound of a twig snapping a few feet away from them.

The sound was deafening in the quiet and they both jumped, causing the brush to twitch momentarily. Their heads turned apprehensively in the direction of the noise, and they were shocked to see a pair of eyes staring right back at them.

In the brush just adjacent to them was a woman, very young in age, barely a woman in Jenny's estimation. Most of her body obscured from the brush that she hid in, all that was visible was her face.

Her expression was one of panic, and her eyes held a crazy glaze to them. Silently, she raised a hand to her mouth, her index finger raised in a "shh" gesture.

"One is coming." She whispered, rather loudly in Jenny's opinion.

Repeating the gesture back to the woman, Jenny again cocked her head, listening for any sound that interrupted the silence that had very quickly become the norm.

After minutes of tense silence, Jenny began to hear the sound of approaching machinery. The mechanical whine of limbs grew closer and closer to their location, and her heart began to hammer so loudly in her ears that she feared it had become audible.

A machine appeared in her view and black spots danced before her eyes. Being this close to a machine, close enough to smell the foreign substance used to "oil" its limbs was overwhelming, and she feared she would pass out from fear. In all that had happened since the beginning of this, nothing had terrified her more than being practically nose-to-nose with the "annihilators," as she was calling them in her head.

Glancing at the woman hiding in the brushes near her, she noted the deer-in-the-headlights look on her face and knew that she was about to make the biggest mistake of her life.

Jenny shook her head adamantly in denial but fight or flight overtook the young woman and with an insanely terrified look toward the duo, she took flight. The young woman barely made it out of the brush before a bright light emitted from the machine erased her from existence.

Jenny wanted to scream. She felt it bubbling from her inner core and forced it back down with considerable effort. Quickly cupping a hand over Nathan's mouth, knowing his feelings mirrored hers, she held them both still and silent.

A different light from the machine, again from the head area, appeared to scan the area, sweeping back and forth. A few minutes of this action, and finding nothing out of the ordinary, which a mechanical groan, it began to move, heading away from them.

Jenny counted their blessings, wondered how many lives they had left and considered every cliché ever written for the situations they had found themselves in. By some miracle, they had survived event after event, and she couldn't imagine why.

She fought back tears that suddenly threatened to overtake her, and continuing to hold Nathan still and silent, they waited long after the sound of machinery passed.

Without a word, she pulled Nathan and their still soaked bags from the brush they hid in. Placing the even heavier burden on her shoulder, she urged Nathan to do the same, and without a backward glance, they began to walk.

The deeper they walked into the wooded area, the thicker it became, and it was soon difficult to gauge the time of day. It was cool, and dark, and considering the hiking they had done since the tornado, somewhat refreshing.

They continued their walk at an unhurried pace until the weight on Jenny's back became unbearable. *I don't know how soldiers do this without complaint*, Jenny thought to herself, and then admonished herself for the absurd thought.

To compare herself to military soldiers was comparing

apples to oranges. They were a very different breed of people, and she knew it. Not that she did not have love and respect for her country, another silly thought considering the current undergoing. She was never athletically inclined, despite her figure, and she had no desire to be.

Jenny's stomach chose that moment to let out a loud growl, and Nathan's quickly followed suit.

Looking around their temporary resting spot, she spied large amounts of fallen branches and decided a small fire to warm some food would not be such a bad idea.

Gathering small bits of wood in her arms, she spied Nathan doing the same out of the corner of her eye. It was apparent he knew what she was about and was anxious to participate if it meant they had food in their stomachs faster.

After they had gathered and arranged a small mound, as Reginald had shown them how to do, she reached in her pack and felt around for the pack of lighters she had pilfered.

The items in her bag were still wet and for a moment, she was disheartened until her fingers found the pack of lighters and realized it was covered in plastic on one side. Hopefully that bit of plastic was enough to protect them from their swim.

Tearing open the package, she flicked the flint on the first lighter and was startled by how bright the spark was. Failing to turn to flame, she tossed it aside and reached for another one. By the third failed one in the pack, the feeling of despair returned. There were only 2 more lighters to try.

With a delicate touch, Nathan stilled her hand from grabbing the next to try, and plucked one from the pack and flicked, and kept flicking. At first, there were the same sparks as the rest, and then blessedly, a flame.

Nathan turned the flame toward their makeshift fire mound, and it caught instantly.

"I guess you really are a Boy Scout now." Jenny whispered. In the small flame, she caught his expression that was half pride, and half sadness.

Jenny wrapped an arm around him and pulled him into a comforting hug.

"I understand," she whispered in his ear. "I'm hurting too, Kid."

Nathan nodded and then pulled away to sit on the opposite side of the fire, his gaze intent on the growing flames.

Stung to the core, but trying her best to not show it, Jenny began to pull items from her bag. Most of the cans were now lacking labels due to the sogginess in her pack. With a shrug, she grabbed three good sized cans and placed them directly into the fire.

While they waited for their mystery feast to heat, Jenny looked at Nathan, her concerns not abating. Although he was responsive, he was not his usual self, and she didn't know how to bring him back.

"Nathan," she began in hushed tones, "Won't you speak to me?"

Nathan looked at her through the fire, his face barely visible, and then he shook his head.

"I'm sorry about Lucky," she cried out, louder than she should have. "I had to keep us safe. And I couldn't help him without endangering us. You see that don't you?"

Nathan nodded, a pain-stricken look on his face at the reminder of his short lived, but beloved pet.

"Then why won't you talk to me?" At this, he shrugged, and his attention returned to the flames of the fire.

Frustration and hurt clenched her heart and she turned her attention to the cans warming in the fire. Grabbing a stick from her side, she poked at them, considering how long they would need to sit in the flames before they were at least a comfortable warmth to consume.

After another chorus of stomach grumbling, she decided they were warm enough and grabbed a damp blanket from Nathan's bag to retrieve them without burning herself. Carefully, she set them to her side, and between them and waited for the cans themselves to cool.

"What are you fools doing!?!" A voice yelled from the silent woods. The voice was so unexpected that Jenny let out a scream of surprise, her hand covering her heart.

Neither Nathan nor Jenny had heard the stranger's approach, which was both shocking and alarming.

"Put that fire out!" The voice demanded as he hurried closer. "Do you want to get yourselves killed? You might as well light a beacon shouting 'here we are!' And stop that screaming, woman!"

With a huff, the gentleman entered their camp and began to kick dirt onto their fire, snuffing out their efforts quickly and efficiently. She could not see his face but could not help but notice that he was extremely tall and athletically built.

Their world was suddenly cast into blackness, and Jenny heard rather than saw Nathan inch his way closer to her protective side.

"What are you doing?" Jenny asked the stranger, shocked by his abrupt behavior.

"Saving your lives." He replied flippantly as he helped himself to a can of their heated food before he hastily left in the same direction he had come.

When Jenny discovered the missing can later, she silently hoped that he choked on it. She considered once again lighting the fire, but after his warning, she decided, pride be damned, he was probably right.

Grabbing two still-damp blankets from Nathan's bag, the pair settled in for the night. Despite the night chill and dampness of his covering, Nathan dropped off to sleep rather quickly, a testament to the difficult day they had.

Jenny's mind hovered over the stranger. He had certainly piqued her interest. When she at last fell into a light sleep, it was to thoughts of a faceless, rude, thieving stranger who intrigued her. *Who was he?*

Chapter 18

Jenny awoke slowly and yawned as she rubbed at her sleep crusted eyes. For a brief moment, she was back in her Manhattan apartment, snug in her bed. And then reality stepped in and she sat up quickly, glancing around her, suddenly as alert as if she had an entire pot of coffee in her gullet.

On her first pass of their makeshift camp, she did not spot anything amiss. On her second, alarm bells rang in her head as she realized that Nathan was not asleep beside her. He was gone.

Her heart hammered in her chest as she hurriedly rose, spinning in circles hoping to spot her little brother.

"Nathan?" She called out quietly, then a little louder. "Nathan!"

No response answered her calls and she darted off hoping she was going the right direction. Within minutes of not locating her ward, she circled back and chose a different direction.

True panic sank in by her third circle and she began to fear the worst. Had one of the machines "erased" him? Had she failed him? How could she live with herself if she had slept while he was erased from existence? How had she slept through his departure? It was neglectful of her to sleep with such lack of awareness. Anything could have happened to him.

Her heart hurt worse by each passing second, her mind racing with all of the possibilities, none of them good. She ran with her hand to her heart, convinced it was going to explode outward at any moment. The pain was excruciating.

After her fourth pass, and moving in yet another direction, she heard a very quiet and distinguishable giggle. Without thought, she sank to her knees in relief at the knowledge that he was still alive.

Closely following that feeling was one of pure anger. How *dare* he worry her like that in these times? Rising to her feet, she trudged noisily toward his location, his giggles her only beacon.

Coming to a clearing, she halted her pace and stared in awe. Sliding down the arm of one obviously broken-down annihilator machine was her young ward.

She was about to approach her brother and drag him down from his makeshift slide when she heard a voice call out angrily from her left.

"Hey, Kid!" The voice yelled in an agitated voice. "Get down from my rig before you get hurt!"

The voice sounded familiar to her, but she couldn't place it until the man stepped into view. It was his abnormally tall height that caught her attention, and she recalled the faceless stranger from the night before.

At the man's yelling, Nathan had halted in place on his perch, and a panicked look crossed his face before he promptly fell from his perch.

Jenny let out a gasp and began running toward her brother, but the stranger beat her to him and caught his little body seconds before it was to collide with the hard ground.

Setting Nathan on his feet, the stranger grasped him by his arms and shook him in exasperation.

"I told you to get off of my rig! Do you know what could have happened, you fool child?"

Giving Nathan one more shake, he set him away from himself and began to inspect the machine.

"You scared him!" Jenny exclaimed accusingly as she drew closer, putting a protective arm around her brother. "He could have broken his neck!"

Noticing her presence at her angry words, the stranger halted his inspection and quickly made his way to her, stopping only when they were toe to toe. Too close for comfort.

The man was *tall*, easily 7 feet in height. He was also

the most athletically built man she had ever seen. He was bulky for his height, but it was blatantly obvious that it was from 100% muscle. She doubted he had an ounce of fat on him. His abs probably had abs, she thought to herself, and was immediately disgusted with herself.

Having to duck so they could be eye to eye, he spoke to her, his tone obviously toned down for her benefit, but his annoyance abundantly clear.

"Have. You. Ever. Heard. Of. Self. Destruct?" he asked her, each word carefully enunciated as if she were hard of hearing, which she was not.

Jenny nodded stupidly, no intelligent words coming to mind.

"I told him to get off my rig for a reason, lady. He was about 1 slide away from blowing himself to pieces. Understand?"

Another dumb, silent nod and she began to doubt her own intelligence. Her IQ suddenly plummeting to that of an amoeba, she could only stare.

Jenny tried not to notice how beautiful his eyes were, even with anger darkening them by the second. They were the most beautiful chocolate brown with flecks of green and gold scattered throughout them. If she could have ever described and written the perfect set of eyes, they would be his.

Suddenly, his words sank in, wrenching her from her ridiculous feminine interest.

"You are one of *them*?" She accused, forcing her brother even further behind her.

"Yes and no," he replied flippantly, straightening his posture to his full height, which suddenly felt quite intimidating. "Same species, race, what have you. Different mission. If you are planning to live much longer, I suggest you two follow me."

"And why should we trust you?" she asked, irritated by his surly attitude.

"What other choice do you have, Lady? I have already saved you both once, him, twice now, you know." Again, with the attitude that grated on her nerves. "Look. I don't have time to debate or argue. Either you come with me, or you die. It is that simple. You have ten seconds to decide."

His declaration hung heavy between them, and she chewed her lip trying to decide if she could trust him. Nathan made the decision for her as he eased himself around her and took the stranger's hand. The stranger looked down at their joined hands in surprise and began to walk. With a weary sigh, she followed them.

The trio backtracked to their makeshift camp and after retrieving their belongings, headed in a different direction. The walk was dizzying and very quickly, Jenny could not even tell which direction they faced anymore.

"Where are we going?" she asked the stranger quietly.

"There is a helicopter pad not far from here. With any luck there is a helicopter on it."

Jenny halted in her tracks and stared at the back of the stranger who continued to walk on, Nathan's hand still securely tucked into his.

"Whoa, whoa, whoa..." she started, "A *helicopter*? Do you even know how to fly one? Won't that make us kind of obvious targets? Can't your people... I don't know... shoot it down?"

Aggravated, the stranger stopped and turned to face her, annoyance written all over his face at having his plan critiqued.

"Yes, a helicopter. I *can* fly one. Yes, they will notice, but we will be moving considerably faster than they can. And no, they cannot shoot us down." he huffed, his agitation crystal clear.

"All I know is I have a location to get to, and I need to be there before this counts down to nothing." he stated, pointing to a watch-looking device strapped to his arm. On it were flashing bars, similar to cell phone signal, and she immediately knew it was a count-down of some sorts.

"What happens when it runs out?" she asked in a whisper, terrified she knew the answer already.

"You don't want to know." With that statement, he turned and began to walk again, Nathan close by his side.

Once again, she was forced to follow, and silence resumed for a while. Inside, she had a million unanswered questions and they churned in her mind, brewing up an impeding storm that was bound to release at some point.

After quite some time, and one shared cold meal since he wouldn't allow a fire, they broke through the trees, once again in a more city-like environment and they quickly approached the helipad that he had promised to direct them to.

A testament to their unfailing luck, there were no machines in sight, and there was indeed a vacant helicopter just sitting there waiting to be of service.

The closer they got to the helicopter, the faster the stranger walked, and the choppier Jenny's breath was until she was nearly hyperventilating. Hysteria gripped her at the idea of getting into that small vessel with a stranger, whose skills she could not be certain of.

"We don't even know your name!" She blurted idiotically, grasping at some straw to delay their impending trip.

Hearing the rising panic in her voice, he sighed, halted and turned toward her, Nathan in tow. He softened his expression, hoping to abate some of her fear.

"My name cannot be pronounced in your tongue. However, those of us in my group have assumed human names so we can be reminded of who we are trying to save." With a pregnant pause, he continued. "The human name I chose is George."

"George?" She repeated, "Why George?"

"I read one of your human books once about monkey named George in a yellow hat. A bit primitive, but I found him amusing and I liked the name. So, I chose George. You may call me that."

"You named yourself after Curious George?" She exclaimed before letting out an indelicate snort which quickly turned to a laugh.

Chapter 19

The most musical sound Jenny had ever heard was the return of Nathan's laugh which had quickly joined her own. Together, they laughed so hard, their abdomens hurt while George looked on in irritated confusion. Tears streamed unchecked down their cheeks and as one would start to calm, the laughter of the other would bring about a new round of mirth.

"He named himself after Curious George." Nathan stated, the first words he had spoken since his kitten had floated away.

"Big, strong, roar-I-am-man, follow me or die... And he named himself after a children's book character!" Jenny replied in humor, slow to catch on to the gravity of the moment.

Nathan's uncontrollable giggles grew, and he dropped to the ground, rolling around while holding his aching sides.

"He's Curious George!" he hollered, bringing about a new round of laughter.

"Enough!" George barked angrily, not enjoying being the butt of a joke that he could not comprehend. The pair sobered at his mandate, and Nathan picked himself up from the ground with the assistance of his sister's hand.

"Nathan!" Jenny suddenly exclaimed in awe. "You spoke! All of this time, and his 'chosen' name was what was needed to make you speak again?"

Nathan's only response was a shrug as he turned toward George, serious once again. George grunted in appreciation of the attentiveness. *At least one of the humans was intelligent,* he thought to himself, before turning to his counterpart.

"If we can be done with the hysteria and amusement, we really need to board the vessel now. I don't think I need to remind you that we are running out of time." he gestured toward the dreaded helicopter. "Get in, both of you, while I check the helicopter over."

Apprehension returning to a smaller degree, Jenny gulped, but hurried to comply, Nathan's hand in hers. They climbed into the helicopter and watched as George circled the helicopter, his face serious as he inspected their ride. A pre-flight check if Jenny remembered the correct term.

Having completed his check to his satisfaction, George climbed up into the pilot seat, Jenny seated beside him and

Nathan in back. Headsets in place so they could hear each other over the roar of their craft, and with a few flips of switches, turns of knobs, all things foreign to Jenny, the helicopter roared to life, and they quickly ascended.

"How do you know how to fly this?" Jenny asked through her headset, trying to mask her fear as the ground moved further and further away.

"I studied all of the manuscripts I could find on primitive vessels. It was not difficult to find." he replied with a shrug.

"How? We are from different planets! It isn't like you would have one just lying around."

"I forget how naïve your species is sometimes." he sighed. "Do you really think that your broadcasts of information are confined to your own planet? Since your species has rediscovered some of its technology, you have been broadcasting to the entire universe. And for quite a while now."

That knowledge, making a little bit of sense to her began to sink in.

"So, we have made ourselves targets then? But why? Why are your people doing this? I don't understand." She was almost yelling in frustration as she ended her statement.

"I don't have time to answer that. I need to concentrate." He dodged, his voice once again gruff, and she knew the conversation had ground to a sudden halt.

She looked into the back to check on Nathan and found him curled up with a blanket that must have been stored back there. In the "quiet" she could hear his gentle snores through the headset as he slept peacefully.

The sound of Nathan snoring so serenely was akin to a lullaby, and after settling as comfortably as she could into her own seat, her eyes began to droop heavily until she could not keep them open a moment longer.

There was something soothing about being in this gruff, odd, stranger's presence and it was a much-needed balm to soothe the horror of the last few days. Within minutes, her snores combined with her brothers, a chorus of temporary contentedness.

***

George, in the pilot seat allowed a brief grin as he peeked at his slumbering passengers. He didn't know what it was about the pair, but as far as humans went, with considerably inferior intelligence, he liked them in a way he was not prepared for.

Even among his own species, one similar to theirs, with only a few genes of difference between them, he was considered a bit of a loner. He did not seek out the companionship of others, and in fact, avoided it as much as possible.

His interests were geared toward soaking up as much knowledge as he could, which he found had no barriers to date. His brain was a sponge that quickly soaked up everything that he read, and he never had to read anything twice. Once it was read, it was committed to memory.

His reading covered a broad spectrum, and in fact, he would indiscriminately read anything that he could get his hands on, so to speak. Because of his knowledge, he was fluent in thousands of foreign languages, could successfully grow any plant on even the barest of planets, and he could fly or drive any kind of machinery with ease from any planet he had researched.

To even his own kind, he was an enigma, his intelligence was so advanced. Intelligence was a trait that he admired in himself, and he was sorely disappointed to find it so lacking in others. Not that he put himself on a pedestal, or thought himself a God, he just wanted companionship that suited his needs, and finding none, had chosen the life of a loner. Until now.

His passengers were as much of an enigma to him as he was to others. It was a discomfiting feeling being on the other side for a change. Both humans had obvious intelligence, a point in their favor, even though it was nowhere near his level. It was their ability to find humor in moments despite their situation that fascinated him.

Watching the pair earlier laughing at his carefully chosen human name, their mirth nearly overwhelming them despite the dangers surrounding them astounded him. It also vexed him to be the source of humor. It was not a comfortable feeling.

Frowning to himself again at this thought, he absentmindedly looked at the gas gauge on their primitive vehicle. His frown deepened as he realized they were not as close to their exit point as he would have liked, but the needle on the gauge was quickly pointing toward empty.

"Damn!" He muttered under his breath in his own tongue, and then repeating it in the English language for good measure.

***

Jenny, on high alert despite her slumber, came awake with a start at his quietly spoken words.

"What's the matter?" she asked quietly as she rose to a seated position. Glancing at Nathan, she made sure he had not been disturbed. His snores confirmed he was still sleeping, and she turned toward George in apprehension.

"We are running out of fuel and are nowhere near where we need to be." he replied evenly without even glancing at her.

"How far away are we?" she asked.

"Far enough for me to be worried." His usual flippant tone returned. "I don't see anywhere safe to land at the moment, and we are leaking fuel. So, I would make sure you have your belt on. It may be a boulder landing."

"Rocky landing." She corrected absentmindedly as she checked to ensure her brother was securely buckled.

"Boulder, rock! Make yourself safe, woman!" He yelled in indignation at her correction. The sudden loud voice startled Nathan awake, and he jolted upright and looked around with panic-stricken eyes before they zeroed in on his sister.

"Sissy?" he asked, fear dripping from that one word. "Is everything okay?"

"It's fine, Nathan," She lied. "We just need to land soon, and it might be a little bumpy."

Hearing her downplay their current situation, George scoffed and was about to make a sarcastic comment until he glanced at Jenny and saw her I-will-kill-you-if-you-say-otherwise look that was familiar among all species.

His mouth snapped shut, all sound cut off, and his eyes focused on their surroundings in hope of a safe place to land. Another glance at the gauge told him he had mere minutes to find a safe spot.

He broke out into a full body sweat, a first for him, and realization slammed into his brain. This feeling that he was having was fear. It was foreign to him as he had never felt it before in his entire existence before now. It coursed through his veins now like a plague and he did not welcome the feeling.

Alarms began to siren loudly in their ears and he gritted his teeth in agitation as he quickly scanned the area. Sweat dripped into his eyes and he swiped it away with the back of his hand.

Below them, lights twinkled, too many lights for his comfort. It was obvious that they were approaching a city, but he was unsure of which one. Human geography was not one of his preferred reading materials, a detail that infuriated him now. That kind of knowledge would have been beneficial at that time.

Silencing the alarms screaming in his ears and avoiding a glance at his passengers so he could not see the fear he expected on their faces, he guided their aircraft toward what seemed like as promising a spot as they were going to get.

"There," he said to no one in particular, "I see a landing spot ahead."

"Is it safe to land?" Jenny asked fearfully.

Somehow, up in the air, even with a pilot she did not know, felt considerably safer than down on the ground with the machines and she was apprehensive thinking about what may await them.

"As safe as it can be." he replied icily, his finger stabbing in the direction of the gas gauge pointedly. "I don't have many options here."

Chapter 20

The landing itself was anticlimactic considering the sequence of events from the past few days. Their craft approached what appeared to be a hospital landing pad, and with admirable expertise, George set them down softly.

Through the headsets that still adorned their ears, there could be heard three simultaneous sighs of relief as the helicopter touched down and the engine shut off. For a long moment, they all sat completely still, each reflecting on their near miss. The moment passed, and as if by silent command, the trio removed their headsets, and scrambled out of the aircraft.

"What now, George?" Nathan asked in a hushed tone.

George ran his hands through his hair, an obvious sign of his agitation. "I'm not sure yet, Kid. I need a moment to think."

"You grownups sure take a lot of time to think." Nathan huffed, threw his bag over his shoulder and began walking with purpose toward the only door leading from the rooftop.

George lightly tapped Jenny's arm, and with a grin, said with admiration, "Precocious little guy, isn't he?"

Jenny rolled her eyes, grabbed her own bag and followed suit.

As they approached the door, George urged his wards behind his back, and he once again assumed command. The door slid open slowly and without a whisper of a sound. He poked his head in and looked around before ushering them inside. He had to duck his head to enter, and Jenny and Nathan tried not to laugh.

"We need to hurry out of here." he whispered, "No doubt we were seen, if not heard and we are sitting ducks if we stay in here."

The stairwell that they found themselves in was dark and had an oppressive, claustrophobic feeling to it. Neither Jenny nor Nathan was willing to argue with George, and in fact, couldn't escape their would-be prison fast enough.

The group hurried down the stairs as quickly as they could with limited visibility. Nathan slipped once, knocking into his sister and nearly propelling her forward. George reacted with insanely fast reflexes and was able to stabilize the pair within seconds. Jenny nodded her thanks, which went unseen as he turned his back and resumed his descent.

What seemed like hours, but was probably in fact

mere minutes, they at last reached an exit. Once more, George urged the others behind him, and he reached for the metal bar handle on the door.

As soon as the door slid open, a loud screeching surrounded them, and strobe lights flashed. George covered his ears and looked at Jenny in horror and confusion. He had obviously not had the pleasure of experiencing an emergency exit before.

"Emergency exit!" Jenny yelled to him.

He shook his head, still confused. Gently prying one of his hands free from his ears, she yelled again, trying to reassure him, despite the alarms.

"Emergency exit! It makes that noise when the door is opened, alerting others in the building that there is an emergency. Let's move before it draws attention to us!"

He blinked at her a few times before her words sank in and he nodded and snapped back into motion.

Looking around, he motioned for them to follow, and dashed from the building. The sun blinded them momentarily, and it took them what could have been costly, precious seconds while they adjusted to the light. Luckily, there were no machines in sight.

As they raced down the streets, hugging the buildings as much as possible, the shrill sounds emitting from the building slowly began to fade into the background. The trio ran until the only sounds that could be heard were their own gasping breaths.

Jenny was the first to give in, the fast pace and weight of her pack weighing her down. Halting, she braced her hands on her knees, hunching over and fighting to regain an even breath. Noticing that she had stopped, George and Nathan returned to her side and an unspoken break ensued.

When their gasping breaths changed to more even breathing, in unison, they sat, leaning their backs on the brick wall of the building they had taken little notice of.

Although her breaths no longer hurt, Jenny's heart still raced from exertion and her mouth had gone bone dry. Of all of the supplies they had grabbed, water had not been at the forefront of her mind, and she mentally kicked herself for her lack of foresight. Glancing at George and Nathan, she noted that they were in the same state as she was, and she began to look around her for a solution to their current predicament.

Across the street from them was a lawyer's office, which she assumed would only suffice for a momentary reprieve if the water was still running. But she knew that she needed to think in long-term, and not immediate.

To the left of the lawyer's office was a small drug store, which offered *some* promise. But she wasn't sure how well stocked it was, being a small drug store. Keeping that business in mind, she continued to scan the stores lining the streets around them. Not many were very promising in their current vicinity. A barber shop, tattoo shop, smoke shop, not exactly helpful for the long run.

She was about to suggest they try the drug store when the light above them flickered, drawing her curiosity. Rising with a silent groan, her muscles still screaming in protest from their mad dash, she backed herself into the street to read the sign of the store they currently resided at. The sign was a mana from heaven. Pete's grocery was flashing, mostly because the "P" light was obviously on its way out.

Despite the sad looking neighborhood it was in, the grocery store appeared to be of a decent size and hope flooded Jenny's heart. Time to restock their supplies, and this time with a bit more smarts, she thought to herself.

Drawing George's attention, Jenny silently pointed to the sign above them. At his nod, they rose as a group, collecting their belongings and headed for the entrance. At the door, George hesitated and let out a frustrated sigh.

"This door isn't going to start screaming too, is it?" he questioned quietly.

"No. This is not an emergency exit, so it should be fine." Jenny replied, sharing a grin with Nathan.

George nodded and pushed at the door, nearly smashing his face into it. He stared at it in consternation and then tried again. A giggle escaped Nathan, and Jenny hurried to shush him, her own grin widening.

"It's a pull door." She explained as she grabbed the handle and held it open.

A blush covered George's face and for a moment, Jenny had to admire how the boyish expression lightened his face, making it more human and adorable. He cleared his throat, his composure returning quickly, much to her regret.

"Well," he barked gruffly, "Let's get to it! What are you two standing there for? Think we have all day?"

The store was not overly large, but was well supplied, Jenny noted. Crouching, she dropped her bag and began to pull all things canned out of it. The cans were much too heavy and too difficult to open. She knew she needed to find lighter, more easily opened items to fill her bag with.

Nathan and George both drifted off in their own directions as she remained crouched and thoughtful. Recent experience had shown her that she needed to be more mindful, not knowing what lay ahead or when they would be able to obtain more supplies again. For that matter, she had no idea for how *long* they were supplying themselves.

George had been less than forthcoming with his information and she was determined to get some answers from him just as soon as she had a chance. She deserved some answers, and she would damn well get them, she thought, frustration temporarily overwhelming her.

Pushing the feeling aside, she rose and began walking

the aisles one-by-one scanning the shelves and carefully selecting her items. Into her bag went small cans of pull top deviled ham, packets of tuna fish, a few apples, a stalk of celery, carrot chips, lunchmeat and cheese (minus the unnecessary condiments), water bottles, a few more items that caught her eye and could easily fit her now considerably lighter bag and topped with a loaf of bread. Feeling quite proud of herself, she headed toward the cash registers and sat on the conveyor belt, waiting for Nathan and George to reappear.

George walked into her sight, an open bag of potato chips in his hand. He reached inside, pulled a chip and popped it into his mouth. The face that he made while he chewed was contemplative and after swallowing, he looked at her.

"What is this? It tastes like processed salt and I'm not sure what." He asked.

"It is exactly what it tastes like." She laughed quietly. "It is processed potato and salt."

He shrugged and then moved down another aisle and out of her sight. Jenny smiled her amusement.

After a few more minutes, Jenny was joined by George and Nathan, and they prepared to leave. Both had brand new backpacks adorning them. Jenny placed a fifty-dollar bill on the register and she and Nathan looked at George expectantly.

"What?" He asked, looking from one to the other.

"You have to put money on the register." Nathan replied.

"Why?" George asked, his confusion and annoyance obvious.

"Because it is the right thing to do." Nathan said, not bothered by George's clipped tone.

Jenny nodded her agreement.

"This is important to you?" George asked sullenly, apparently not thrilled at the idea of parting with his alien currency.

Both heads nodded and he heaved a sigh before pulling a strange looking coin from his pocket and depositing it on top of Jenny's bill.

"Probably more than this is worth." He grumbled as they headed for the door.

Chapter 21

After quietly exiting the building, the trio halted and ears perked, strained to hear even the slightest sound that was out of place. Having heard none, they began to walk onward. Occasionally, George would stop by one of the cars lining the streets and test the handle before moving on. Jenny was intrigued by his behavior but kept silent. By the tenth or so car, she couldn't help herself.

"What are you doing?" She asked in a whisper.

"I am trying to find us a car." He replied flippantly as if her question was an ignorant one.

"But we have passed quite a few cars." she replied, ignoring his attitude. "Why haven't you checked them all? I have only seen you check a few."

"Because we need a fast car." He huffed in annoyance at her questioning. "Doesn't anybody leave their cars unlocked here?"

Taking a page from his book, she shrugged indignantly. His attitude annoyed her. He treated her and Nathan as though they were beneath him and as ignorant as infants. It irked her to be made to feel so insignificant and small. Her face reddened as her anger rose and she stomped on ahead of him.

In truth, she realized that some of her anger was misplaced. It wasn't just him that she was angry with. She was infuriated with her lack of understanding of the situation that they were in. She didn't know the full extent of the what's or the why's and that irritated her and gave her such an overwhelming sense of helplessness that it nearly brought tears to her eyes. Stopping in her tracks, she turned to confront George, anxious for some explanations.

"*Why*?" she asked, her voice breaking. He understood the meaning behind her single uttered demand but shook his head in denial. He would reveal nothing, and she knew it.

"You claim you are on 'our side' but won't explain to me why?" Her voice became shrill with his denial and hysteria once again began to bubble up inside of her, aching to boil over at the slightest provocation.

Intent on silencing her rather loud exclamations, he leaned down, yanked her into his arms and kissed her. The kiss affected him far more than he had expected. He had intended to only press a hard kiss to her lips, but she had opened her mouth in surprise and his tongue greedily rushed inside tangling with her own. The kiss nearly brought him to his knees. Hers too, he noted, arrogantly pleased as he pulled back and noted the glazed expression in her eyes. He wanted to kiss her again and couldn't for the life of him figure out why.

The fog slowly lifted from Jenny, and she stared at him in shock.

"Why did you do that?" she asked breathlessly.

"To silence you." He replied with a shrug as if the moment hadn't robbed him of his senses as well.

Jenny's face burned red with either embarrassment or anger. He wasn't sure which, and he instantly regretted his words. The slap caught him by surprise although deep inside he knew he deserved it.

"Don't *ever* do that again!" She growled; her voice low but menacing.

She spun away from him, and her gaze settled on the startled expression on her brother's face. She had forgotten he was even there! She grabbed his hand and began walking on. He followed in a stunned silence. The sound of George's footfalls close behind them was reassuring even though Jenny was angry with him.

"No promises." He stated a few minutes later while once again taking the lead.

It took a full minute for Jenny to realize what he was talking about, and another furious blush covered her cheeks.

The trio walked on in silence, George occasionally

testing the handle on cars that they passed. Each was lost in their own thoughts. Jenny was wondering what in the hell was wrong with her to accept the alien's kiss, and admittedly, participate in it. George wondered how long it would take to find a suitable car, and why they hell these people didn't leave their cars unlocked. Nathan considered what he had seen, and to his childish eyes, he was intrigued. Would George be his new brother?

So deep in thought, none of them heard the machines until it was almost too late. The sound of familiar mechanical whines broke the silence and George held up a hand, urging his companions to halt.

Their ears cocked, they tried to judge the distance of the machines only to realize that the sounds were too close for comfort and approaching their location with considerable speed. To their left, the machine appeared to be a couple of blocks away. On their right, the sounds were much closer.

Jenny's heart pounded so hard in her chest that the sound reverberated in her ears. In desperation, she spun around like a child's play top, frantically searching for a usable hiding spot. That action only succeeded in making her dizzy as she spun so fast that she couldn't actually focus on her surroundings.

George and Nathan were much more controlled in their reactions. Nathan looked up at George expectantly, knowing George would find a way out of this predicament.

Latching onto Jenny's hand, George stilled her and scanned the street. The sounds were getting louder and much closer, but he didn't panic. His focus was on the cars lining the street. Glancing at each one, he gauged their speed capabilities and discarded one after another as potential getaway vehicles until his eyes zeroed in on one that he thought just might do.

Half of a block ahead of them was a brand-new Dodge Charger Hellcat in indigo blue. George blinked in surprise at the beautiful car and hoped like hell the keys were inside of it. It would be a shame if he had to hot-wire such a beauty. He knew from his extensive reading that the Hellcat was a very fast ride, and he was almost giddy with excitement.

Grabbing onto Nathan's hand and gripping Jenny's tighter, he raced toward the car. They were nearly to the car when one of the machines came into view and George knew they were out of time. Either extreme luck or extreme death was about to be their fate and he sincerely hoped for the former.

George did not slow his pace as they approached the car and the three of them slammed into the side of it and bounced off. The force of their bodies dented the side and George groaned internally at the damage.

The machine had not spotted them, and they used the car as a barrier, protecting them from sight. Reaching up, George grabbed the door handle and pulled. The door opened easily. He nodded to Jenny, and she scrambled into the car and over the gear shift, keeping her body as low as possible. Next was Nathan's turn. The driver's seat was pushed forward, and Nathan scrambled into the back.

"Scoot to the other side, Nathan." George whispered. "My legs are too long for this car, and I'd squish you."

Nathan hurried to comply and after pushing the seat back as far as it could go, George and Jenny searched for keys. Under the seat seemed a reasonable, but empty hiding spot. The console was the same. George was just about to give up and hot-wire the car when Jenny pulled on the sun visor and the keys dropped into his lap.

"Everybody buckle-up." George commanded, the key hovering in his hand next to the ignition. "Once I start this car up, we are going to fly out of here as fast as I can get it to go."

With the complete lack of traffic escape seemed plausible, except for the machine that was directly in front of them a block ahead. George hoped that Jenny wouldn't ask his plan because he was confident her hysteria would return, and he did not have time to calm her. It was now or never.

His foot on the clutch, he jammed the key into the ignition, started the engine and threw the car into gear. Changing gears furiously, they sped toward the machine blocking their way. The machine turned toward them at the sound.

"What are you *doing*?" Jenny screamed hysterically as she covered her eyes. "We need to get away!"

"We *are* getting away!" he yelled back. "I can't exactly turn this thing around and we need speed to get away! We are going under."

With that half-explanation, he changed gears again and before the machine could focus on them, they launched beneath the legs of it, the roof of their car scraping on the undercarriage. Relief flooded him as they raced away, putting distance between them and the machine at a startlingly fast rate. He *really* liked the car.

Once they were in the clear and the machine was no longer in sight, he grinned like a fool and glanced at his passengers. Nathan was turned in his seat and was watching out of the back window as buildings rushed by like a blur. Their quick and risky escape did not seem to faze him and his complete trust in George was humbling. Jenny on the other hand was still tense with her eyes covered and her breath coming in pants. George patted her knee to sooth her and she peeked at him from the side of her hand.

"It's okay. We made it. They are far behind us now." He crooned softly as if to calm a frightened child.

She did *not* want to be soothed and she was certainly not a child! Her hands dropped to her lap and her temper burst. Suddenly she was smacking his arm with alternating hands, and she couldn't seem to stop herself.

"What in the hell!" She yelled in his ear. "You could have killed us!"

"I had it under control." He winced at her sharp stinging slaps and began to growl as they continued. "I swear, Lady, if you don't stop smacking me, I am going to open your door and shove you out."

Nathan turned at the threat and watched curiously as Jenny slowly regained her composure. With a scowl on her face, she ceased her blows and sank back into her seat.

"Jenny." She grumbled.

"What?"

"Every time you address me, you call me 'Lady.' My name is Jenny."

"I know." He replied, his grin returning. "And that's Nathan in the back. Why don't you try to rest '*Lady*.' You may have to take over driving at some point."

Jenny bit back a biting retort at his mocking and turned toward her window. She glanced out but wasn't really seeing. She had an overwhelming urge to cry, and she sniffled as a few tears escaped.

"It's okay, Jenny." Nathan whispered loudly in her ear, his small hand stroking her shoulder. "George won't let anything happen to us. He will keep us safe."

Chapter 22

Jenny woke with a start. Disoriented for a moment, she looked around, not knowing where she was. Memory flooded her and she tensed. She was in the passenger seat of their pilfered car. The interior was as dark as outside her window, the only visible light coming from the headlights.

"How long was I asleep?" She wondered aloud.

"For quite a while." George replied in a hushed tone. She glanced at his shadowed features and then her gaze moved to the back of the car. "He's still sleeping."

"Where are we?" she asked just as quietly.

"I'm not sure. It's hard to read the signs when you are driving so fast. We are close though. We made up some time while you were sleeping. Are you hungry? I am."

Her stomach grumbled loudly in response, and she reached for her bag to pull some food out for them. She made him a thick deviled ham sandwich and handed it to him. He thanked her and took a huge bite. She turned to wake Nathan so she could feed him as well, but he stopped her.

"No." he said around the mound of food in his mouth. "Let the kid sleep. He will wake if he gets too hungry."

Jenny shrugged, knowing he was right and turned her attention to making her own sandwich. Beside her, George groaned in bliss as he shoved the remainder of his sandwich into his mouth. Her earlier aggravation laid to rest during her extended nap, she could only grin.

"Another?" she asked, unable to keep the amusement from her voice.

"Yes, please."

Setting her own in her lap, she made him another and handed it to him. He devoured the second one as quickly as the first but declined a third. Shrugging, she picked her own up and had to restrain her own groan of pleasure after the first bite.

After downing her sandwich nearly as quickly as George had done, she wiped her fingers on her pant leg and turned to look out the window. Now that her eyes had adjusted to the darkness, she realized it wasn't exactly pitch-black out, but it was close.

The moon was high in the sky but overcast. Trees whizzed by ghostly blurs in the dim moonlight. There weren't any buildings that she could see, and it was obvious that they were well away from anything resembling a city. Oddly, this comforted her.

"You said we are close?" she asked, turning back to face George.

"Yes."

"How do you know which direction to go?"

"I just do."

"But, how?" she persisted.

"Coordinates." he replied, knowing full well his brief answers were beginning to irritate her again.

The less she knew, the better. Not receiving any actual answers, she huffed out a sigh and sat back in her seat.

Silence resumed and lasted for a good long while before Nathan awoke. He was given a sandwich which he devoured as quickly as they had. Satisfied with that need, he turned to the next demanding one.

"George, I have to go to the bathroom." he implored.

"Alright. We can make a quick stop in the woods here."

"Do you think it's safe?" Jenny asked concerned.

George rolled his eyes and nodded before slowing the car and pulling off to the side of the road. One by one they climbed out of the vehicle groaning from the stiffness in their limbs.

As they stretched their sore muscles, George laid out the ground rules in an authoritative tone. No wandering and they were too all stay within shouting distance of each other while they sought their privacy. Nathan squirmed throughout the speech while he waited for a moment to speak.

"Sissy?" he whispered with embarrassment. "Do you have toilet paper?"

"No. I didn't think to grab any." she replied.

"But Sissy! I have to *pooh!*" He wailed helplessly and George began to laugh before taking his hand.

"Come on little man. I'll show you the outdoor man's toilet paper."

Jenny stifled a giggle as she thanked him for his assistance before setting off in the opposite direction to satisfy her own need. *Outdoor man's toilet paper.* She did giggle then.

She didn't walk far. The woods were just off the side of the road, and she ducked behind a large tree within eyesight of their car. After finishing her needs, she strolled back to the car lost in thought.

A warm feeling enveloped her, and it took her moments to recognize what it was. Peace. They had so little of that lately that the feeling was becoming foreign. Terror, desperation and anger she was familiar with. Peace had seemed a dream of the past. She decided to enjoy it while it lasted.

She waited by the car for a few more minutes enjoying the quiet stillness before she heard the guys returning. Nathan had an ear-to-ear smile on his face, and she didn't have to wonder long.

"I'm a Boy Scout *and* an outdoors man now!" he proudly exclaimed. George laughed at the announcement as he ruffled the boy's hair.

"That you are, Kid. Are you two ready to go now? We are close but still have a way to go."

The trio climbed back into the car with only a brief delay as George groaned over the scratched roof of the car. *Such a shame to mark up such a beautiful car.* He thought to himself.

Back on the road, the mood was light and although it was the middle of the night, Nathan was full of energy and questions. He bounced in his seat in the back as he questioned George about his own home planet.

"What is your planet like, George?"

After a moment of thought, he replied. "It is pretty similar to yours, Nathan. Except ours is in much better condition."

"How so?"

"Well, we don't pollute our planet with trash and chemicals. We take very good care of it."

"What does pollute mean?" Nathan asked in a puzzled voice.

"It's like when people throw their trash on the ground." Jenny interjected.

"Oh!" he responded. "But we don't do that, do we, Jenny? Our trash *always* goes in the trash can!"

"Yes, it does." she replied. Turning to George, she

asked, "What is happening to our people? Where did they go?"

George shook his head, again refusing to answer. Disgruntled, she scowled at him. *Sure, he can answer a child's questions, but not mine.* Nathan peppered him with more and more questions about his planet and Jenny only partly listened.

Looking out the window, she watched as more and more trees sped by. The scene was hypnotic combined with the chatter in the car, and she soon found her eye lids getting heavy again despite her long earlier nap. She rested her head on the window and let the sound of George's husky voice lull her into a doze. She had nearly fallen asleep when she felt George's hand cover her knee.

"Hey. You okay over there?" he asked quietly.

"Yeah," she replied sleepily. "I was just dozing off for a minute."

She was about to sit up straighter in her seat when he gently patted her knee.

"Get some rest. I will wake you if I need to."

Nathan and George continued to chatter in hushed tones and within minutes she was sound asleep and snoring, much to George's amusement.

He kept his hand on her knee, liking the feeling of touching her too much to remove it. It amazed him how good it felt inside to just touch another being. Or maybe it was just her. He had never had the desire or the need to do so with his own kind.

Smiling, he drove past the break in the woods and entered a tunnel that would take them through the mountain in front of them. He was still smiling when they reached the other side. He never saw it coming.

Chapter 23

Exiting the tunnel on the other side, George was shocked to see a mechanical arm swing out and slam into the side of the car. Metal crunched on metal and the car was thrown high into the air. Over and over the car spun and time seemed to freeze as he awaited the dreaded descent.

Beside him and behind him he heard their screams of terror, but he couldn't make himself look. He couldn't seem to let his grip of the steering wheel go either. All around them their bags and items from them bounced around, ceiling to floor and back again. But he couldn't see, couldn't move. He was paralyzed with fear for the first time in his life.

After what seemed like an eternity, the car slammed into a tree and dropped onto its wheels. The impact forced George's head forward and his face connected with the steering wheel. Unconsciousness was instantaneous.

"George! Jenny! George! Jenny!" A voice hollered in his ear, stirring him.

He was slow to recognize the voice through the fog and pain in his head. The voice continued to call, desperately pleading. It was the sorrow and desperation that snapped him out of it.

George opened his eyes to see Nathan perched on the center console, his face close to his own. The look of concern on his little face tore at his heart. Peering past him, he saw that Jenny was still unconscious.

"How long was I out?" he asked Nathan.

"Only a few minutes. I can't get Jenny to wake up though."

"Alright. Let's climb out my side and we will see if we can wake her."

Climbing out and moving toward the other side of the car, they surveyed the damage and were amazed how extensive it was. It was a miracle that they had survived, and George hurried toward Jenny's door, fearing that she was more injured than he had suspected.

As they neared her severely dented door, they heard Jenny groan, and both let out a sigh of relief. Her window had smashed in during the impact and George used his sleeve to dislodge some of the more jagged pieces.

Jenny opened her eyes and looked around in confusion as George gently brushed pieces of glass from her hair. She didn't appear to be injured, much to his relief.

"Are you alright?" George asked in concern.

"I think so," She replied as her eyes became more focused. "Are you?"

George had a large welt on his forehead where he had connected with the steering wheel. Although it was not bleeding, his head pounded.

"I am fine." He lied, brushing away her concerns.

"What do we do now?"

"For the moment, let's just worry about getting you out of the car. Your door is pretty dented. Can you climb to the driver's side?"

Jenny tried to shift herself to the other seat and quickly realized that she was unable to. Her right leg was pinned between the seat and the door. A fleeting moment of panic took her as she realized that she was stuck. Recognition of the seriousness of her situation came with resignation.

"I can't," she replied softly. "My leg is pinned. You guys will have to go on without me. Just promise me that my brother will be taken care of."

Nathan shouted in protest and George's face contorted in anger at her declaration. There was no way they were leaving her behind!

"If you think we are leaving you, then you are daft, Woman!" George growled.

"There isn't much time, and I am *stuck*! The obvious conclusion is that you guys carry on and make it!" she growled back, ignoring the now pleading Nathan.

"Look, Jenny," George began to state his absurd case.

"I care about you. I don't know what this 'love' is that your kind speaks of, but if it means that I cannot abide the thought of leaving you behind, then maybe it's that. I can't bear the thought of not seeing you again. You and your brother mean too much to me. So, deal with it, Woman! We are getting you out of that car and you are going with us if I have to carry you the rest of the way!"

Jenny gaped at him in stunned silence. She knew she should say something back, to tell him that she cared about him too, but she was rendered speechless by his fervent declaration. He nodded at her, as if he understood exactly what she hadn't said. Nathan, who had been near tears moments prior looked like his face would split from his grin.

"Stand by the end of the car, Nathan." George ordered gently before turning his attention to the dented door. He considered the problem for a brief moment before grabbing onto it by the handle and the window. Anger, fear, and frustration gave him Herculean strength, and with a very loud growl, he wrenched the door away and tossed it to the side. Jenny couldn't help but be impressed by the feat of strength.

As soon as her leg was freed, pain exploded in her leg and Jenny grimaced and cried out involuntarily. She grabbed at her sore leg, running her hands over it, feeling for breaks. Finding her leg still intact despite the excruciating pain, she let out a breath that she didn't know she had been holding.

"Is it broken?" George asked worriedly.

"I don't think so. But it really hurts." she replied.

George knelt next to her and offered a hand of assistance. She took his hand and began to rise from the car before her leg collapsed, refusing to accept her weight. Before she could hit the ground, she found herself swung up into his arms and cradled against his chest.

"I will carry you." He stated in a voice that left no room for argument. "Come, Nathan. We are almost there."

Jenny took in their surroundings and almost let out a groan as she realized that they were once again going to have to trek through a wooded area. She was beginning to dislike trees and bushes.

Nathan dutifully followed George into the woods and the now customary silence resumed. The only sound that could be heard was the sound of their feet gently pattering over dried leaves and twigs. Jenny was once again struck by the eeriness of the lack of sound. It made her shiver.

"Are you cold?" George asked her in a whisper. She shook her head against his chest but did not explain. He did not ask her to.

The woods were dark, the moon barely illuminating their surroundings and then only through the thinnest of trees. It made their travel slow going. Jenny had never been one to fear the dark, but as they walked further into the woods, she began to stiffen in apprehension. George felt her stiffen against him and immediately tried to sooth her.

"It is going to be okay, Jenny. Do you trust me?"

"I know," she replied. "And yes, of course I do."

"Then relax. I won't let anything happen to you. Or Nathan."

She forced herself to relax in his arms, and in the dark felt, rather than saw Nathan touch her arm in a gesture of comfort.

"George will keep us safe." Nathan whispered.

"I know." She said and smiled to herself over the absolute faith her little brother had in the man cradling her so gently in his arms.

On they walked, occasionally stumbling over a discarded branch until it became impossible to see even their own hands in front of their faces. It was the epitome of pitch black.

"We will stop here for the night." George stated, calling a halt to their hike. "It would be dangerous to keep going."

"Do we have enough time to stay here for the rest of the night?" Jenny asked.

"Yes." He replied without embellishment.

George settled himself on the ground with his back to a tree and shifted Jenny into his lap. Her head rested on his shoulder and her legs were sprawled out. She wrapped her arms around his waist and was amazed by how trim he was despite his bulk. Her leg throbbed in pain, distracting her, and she knew without even looking that it was swollen. She reached a hand up to his face to feel the welt on his forehead had swollen to the size of an egg.

"That must hurt." she whispered; her touch delicate as a hummingbird's wings. He caught her hand in his own and swallowed at the emotion choking all words from his throat.

"I am fine." He said in a husky voice. "Why don't you try to get some sleep?"

George did not release her hand but continued to hold it in his much larger hand. He felt Nathan curl into his side and with his other arm, he wrapped it protectively around the boy. A feeling of contentment and rightness threatened to overwhelm him. He couldn't help but feel like this was the moment he had waited his entire life for. These people were where he belonged. Light snores from both his shoulders made his smile as he marveled at how quickly the pair could fall asleep. Minutes later, he felt his own growing weariness and his eyes became heavy. Shifting to a more comfortable position, he dozed.

Chapter 24

Jenny opened her eyes and gently stretched her limbs with cat-like grace. Pain in her leg startled her until recollection entered her sleep-fogged mind. It was certainly sore, but not to the extent that it had been hours before. She was sure that some of the swelling was down as the muscles did not feel as stiff and tight as they had been.

Peering up at George's face, now visible in the dim morning light, she was embarrassed to see him watching her intently. A blush covered her cheeks.

"Good morning," he said in a sleep-husky voice. "How are you feeling?"

Her blush intensified as she realized she was still cradled in his arms and that she had slept so peacefully in his arms. She had never slept with a man before and found the act profoundly intimate.

"I feel alright. My leg is still sore, but not as bad as it was. How is your head?"

George laughed at the blush staining her cheeks and

guessed the reason for it. He thought she was adorable just as she was at that moment.

"My head is fine. But my bladder is full to bursting. I didn't want to wake you, so I have been waiting. You are adorable when you snore by the way."

Jenny scooted off his lap so he could get up and let out an indignant snort. "I do not snore."

"Yes, you do." He stated, as he rose and stretched, his shirt pulling tight over his muscular chest.

She swore he had intentionally flexed just to get a rise out of her. It worked. She was so distracted by his mouth-watering form that she didn't immediately notice Nathan's absence. George did though and a look of concern flashed across his face.

"Where is Nathan?" he wondered aloud.

Startled by the question, she looked around for the boy. *Not again*, she thought to herself. She refused to panic and was sure her brother would appear at any moment.

"Maybe he had to go to the bathroom too."

George nodded his agreement and offered to look around as he found a spot to relieve himself in privacy. Jenny found herself alone and uncomfortable as her own bladder brought attention to itself. She glanced around and found a long branch within reach that she could use as a crutch. She was sure that although her injured leg was feeling better, it would not support her full weight.

Awkwardly, she rose using the makeshift crutch to

help her up from the hard ground. Looking in the direction that George had gone, she went in the opposite direction. She did not go far and kept their campsite in view in case Nathan returned. Ducking behind a bush, she made quick work of emptying her bladder and then ambled her way back to where she had been seated minutes before.

A few long minutes later, she heard movement in the brush and turned to see George returning. Nathan was not at his side and fear began to niggle its way into her heart.

"You couldn't find Nathan?" she asked, and he shook his head.

"No. And I am not sure if we should go looking for him or remain here in case he returns." His consternation at the dilemma was apparent. He swiped a hand through his hair in a nervous gesture she had come to recognize.

"Maybe we should give him a few more minutes and then if he isn't back, we can search in grids close to here."

George agreed with her plan and sat down beside her to wait. Neither said a word as they listened intently for sounds of the boy's return. A few minutes felt like an eternity as they sat there unmoving and hearing nothing. With no sign of the boy, George rose and held out a hand to Jenny, helping her to her feet. He handed her the crutch and nodded in the direction of his choosing.

"I suppose we can start by looking in this direction. We can go for a bit and then come back here and choose another direction if we don't find him. I almost hope he went this way since it is the direction we need to go."

"How do you know that?" she asked him curiously. "You seemed to know which direction last night too. How do you do that?"

"Last night I used the constellations to guide me. As far as today, I don't know. I have always had a very good sense of direction." he shrugged.

She didn't question him further and they walked on at a snail's pace due to her awkward gait. Both called softly for Nathan. His lack of response was making them both nervous. Jenny swore when they found him, he was getting a stern lecture about wandering off! *If we ever find him*, she thought in despair.

They walked for a while in the direction he had chosen and after not locating Nathan, they returned to their campsite and chose another direction. They made the trip three more times before they began to feel disheartened. On their fifth trip, they were about to turn around when they finally heard a soft reply to their calls.

Relief almost brought Jenny to her knees and might have if George hadn't steadied her. Once glance at him assured her that he was not unaffected either. They headed toward Nathan's voice, periodically calling out to him until his voice became louder and closer.

They broke out into a clearing with a stream running through it and found Nathan sitting at the water's edge.

He had his feet in the water, which had to be frigid, but he didn't seem to mind. He had a grin on his face and did not appear to comprehend the scare that he had given the couple.

"Nathan!" she began to scold the child. "You can't just wander off! What if we hadn't found you? What if one of *them* had found you? What if you were hurt? Don't you understand? Anything could have happened to you, and we wouldn't *know!*"

Jenny ended her tirade as her brother's face turned from abashed to apologetic. She almost felt bad for yelling at him but refused to take the words back. Her brother had terrified her with his thoughtless action!

George had looked like he wanted to silence her as she raged but kept himself quiet. In truth, he could have added a word or two of his own, but tears filled Nathan's eyes and he knew that his intrusion would push the boy over the edge. Jenny had stressed the point accurately, albeit loudly and harshly.

"I'm sorry, Sissy." Nathan whispered. "I didn't mean to scare you. I had to go potty and then I found this spot. The water looked pretty, and I was thirsty too, so I sat down here. The water doesn't taste too bad! And it feels really good on my feet! I was feeling dirty too."

Jenny hadn't realized her own thirst until Nathan mentioned it and she glanced warily at the water. Her throat was dry, and her throat ached from yelling her displeasure. She watched George kneel on the bank and cupping his hands, he began to drink. He repeated the action until he had slaked his own thirst and then wiped his mouth with his arm.

"He is right. It doesn't taste too bad. Have a drink, Jenny."

"I don't know." she hesitated. "It could have parasites or something."

Nathan and George both rolled their eyes at her apprehension and then had themselves another drink.

"Suit yourself." George said with a grin, purposefully slurping the water from his palms.

Not amused by his childish antics, she moved to the water's edge and had a tiny sip. Discovering that they were correct about the taste, she dipped her hands for more and took large swallows. The guys shared an I-told-you-so look and it was her turn to roll her eyes.

Suddenly feeling rather impish herself, Jenny turned toward the still crouching George and tried to nudge him into the water. She would have better luck moving a brick wall and his look of surprise was the last thing she saw before she fell into the water herself.

Jenny was sputtering when she rose from the waist deep water and barely had time to voice a complaint before Nathan let out a whoop of delight and cannonballed himself into the water next to her, splashing her in the face. She wiped the moisture away and mock-glared at

George as he let out a bark of laughter. Nathan rose to the surface and grinned at George.

"Come in, George!" he called in delight. "The water is cold, but it feels *good!*"

George shook his head in denial but didn't argue as the soaking wet pair reached for his hands and dragged him in with them. He didn't put up a fight and Jenny knew that was deliberate. He was letting them pull him or they wouldn't have been able to budge him otherwise.

George made a big show of being dragged in, and a very large slash considering the shallowness of the stream. Jenny swiped at the surface and splashed him in the face in retribution and a splash fight ensued. Nathan was giggling as he joined in and the three of them enjoyed those moments of joy and pleasure. Jenny couldn't remember the last time she had that much fun.

She sank into the waist deep water and allowed herself to float. The weightlessness and coolness of the water soon eased some of the throbbing from her sore leg.

"I'm going to get you!" Nathan yelled as he dove under the water and rocketed himself toward Jenny. He swam like a fish, and she let out a cry of surprise when he gently pinched her leg. He resurfaced behind a grinning George.

The three of them played in the water for quite a while. They laughed so much and so hard that their sides ached as they finally departed the stream. In unison, they flopped down on their backs at the bank and struggled to catch their breath.

"We need to be moving soon." George stated somberly. Reality crashed through the joyous mood and popped it like a fragile bubble. Jenny let out a sigh of regret, knowing that he was right. Their moment, as enjoyable as it had been, was over.

"Can't we stay a little longer?" Nathan pleaded, obviously as unwilling to let go of the moment of levity as she had been.

"Sorry, Kid."

They stayed by the bank until their water-logged clothes had dried to a slightly uncomfortable dampness before they set off on their way again.

"Which way, George?" Nathan chirped. George nodded in the appropriate direction and Nathan took the lead. "Follow me!"

The foliage was thick and although they estimated it was around mid-morning, their surroundings still had a dark and grey gloom to it. They strolled at Jenny's pace to accommodate her injury and in truth it felt like they were crawling backwards, so slow was the pace.

Her leg throbbed from the effort of putting one foot in front of the other and she stumbled from time to time, causing the ache to worsen until she was leaning heavily on her crutch. George was right by her side to assist her every time.

Their stomachs began to grumble and as much as she tried to ignore the feeling, Jenny began to regret not retrieving their bags from the car. She sincerely hoped that they stumbled upon something edible along their way as she knew George would never allow them to return to the car. It would cost them more time than they could spare, and they had already wasted much of it playing in the stream. She knew that Nathan and George felt the same and none voiced a single complaint.

A weariness had settled upon them, erasing their earlier pleasant moods. Noting Jenny's struggles, George was about to demand a halt to give her a respite when, in boredom, Nathan raced ahead and plowed headfirst into a clearing. And a machine.

Chapter 25

Jenny let out an audible gasp and latching onto her brother's arm, forced him behind her back. Her first instinct was to run, but she knew they would not be able to outrun it. Her next was to stay as still as possible and hope that they were not noticed. That hope was not realized, however, and the blood rushed from her face as the machine pivoted to face them.

George moved to place himself in front of the pair. His stance was a protective one. His posture demanded that the owner of the machine go through him before they get to his companions.

If Jenny wasn't so scared, she might have found the action admirable and sweet even. A knot formed in her throat, and she fought the urge to cry. They had come so far, to have it end now was unthinkable. She didn't exactly know what would happen when they would have reached their destination, only that salvation beckoned. Now it was gone. She stared at the machine from over George's shoulder and waited for something to happen. Anything to end the ridiculous stalemate they appeared to be in.

What she could only describe as a hatch suddenly popped open and the most beautifully striking woman that she had ever seen slipped from the machine.

Her movement was fluidly cat-like as she hastily approached them. She was tall and trim, which seemed to be the norm for their species. Long, midnight black tresses trailed behind her and as she neared, her deep blue, almost iridescent eyes shone with recognition. The woman was so captivatingly beautiful that Jenny felt a pang of jealousy. She felt like the ugliest of hags standing before such a vision.

"George!" The vision purred. "I was beginning to fear that you wouldn't make it! I was positively *heartbroken* with worry!"

The woman trailed her hand down his arm as she made her dramatic statement and Jenny had to resist the urge to slap it away. George grunted and turned to pull Jenny and Nathan to his side so he could make introductions.

"Cat, this is Jenny and Nathan. Guys, this is Cat."

Cat, Jenny thought, *what an appropriate name for such a creature.* She felt sure that any moment claws would retract from the woman's perfect fingers and sink into her face. The look on Cat's face was a possessive one that evidenced her displeasure. Her features changed to a sultrier one as she ignored the pair and focused yet again on George.

"George," she cooed, "Camp is not far from here, would you like a ride? I'd be happy to squeeze you in. I've been on patrol and am due back shortly."

George denied her offer, gesturing pointedly to Jenny and Nathan.

"I think it would be a little too cramped in there with the four of us."

Cat pouted and then glared at Jenny with obvious disdain. Jenny felt herself turning red with anger at the uncalled-for attitude and would have remarked had George not slipped an arm around her shoulders, taking the bite out of her anger.

"They can't walk?" Cat asked quietly.

Jenny's anger was renewed, and George's ignited. In an unfamiliar language that sounded much like gibberish to Jenny, he began to yell, his face red with anger. Jenny had no idea what he was saying, but it was obvious by his body language and tone that he was furious.

Cat shouted back in the same language until, resigned, she pouted again and returned to her machine. The hatch hissed as it closed, and she left.

"*What* was that all about?" Jenny asked in confusion.

"Don't worry about it." George grumbled, still irritated by the confrontation with Cat.

Despite their mission to save as many humans as

possible, she had been offended by the presence of his companions. It was disconcerting and made him wonder just how dedicated to their cause she was. He shook his head, freeing his thoughts.

"Which way to camp?" Nathan asked quietly, not entirely oblivious to the tension in the air around him.

George didn't respond to the question but began to walk. Jenny and Nathan hurried to follow, exchanging wary glances. George's mood was volatile, and they trailed him at a lengthy distance, not that he was observant enough to realize he was leaving them behind anyway. He moved like a man on a mission, nearly leaving them behind before realizing he was doing so.

"Sorry." He muttered as he backtracked and met pace with them. "She said camp is about a mile from here. We should reach it soon. When we get to camp there will be food and a warm fire."

George didn't say anything more and Jenny and Nathan didn't ask any further questions. They sensed his less than stellar mood and did not wish to upset him further.

"Camp" as it turned out was a large clearing in what Jenny guessed to be the middle of the woods. Wandering throughout camp were far more people than Jenny expected to see. There had to be at least 50 people wandering about camp. Considering the lack of contact with others as of late, the sight took Jenny's breath away.

Children raced around without a care in the world while the elderly lounged beneath makeshift tents. People of all ages mingled at what looked like individual campsites. The sight was so foreign but familiar to Jenny that her chest tightened with remembrance.

At first it was hard to distinguish between human and alien. Both species were so similar genetically, but she soon came to observe that their species had a more "beautiful" look to them as if they had been scientifically enhanced.

"Beautiful, aren't they?" A voice whispered behind her.

Turning, Jenny noted the voice belonged to a young woman, around her own age, who could be defined as beautiful herself. She was tall and lean with long chestnut hair and milk chocolate eyes. George was startled by her sudden appearance and Jenny just nodded her agreement.

"I am Leela Green." The young woman said as she introduced herself. "Would you like me to show you guys around?"

"I'm Jenny Lowe, and this is my brother, Nathan." Jenny said, pointing to her brother and then to George. "And this is George."

"Wait. *The* Jenny Lowe? As in the author Jenny Lowe?" Leela squealed in excitement as if she had just met her favorite actor and was suddenly star-struck. "I have read *all* your books! You are so talented!"

Jenny blushed a deep red and turned to glance at

George who was staring at her with a look of admiration and awe. His mouth opened and closed as if he was about to say something but couldn't quite get the words out. Blushing even deeper, Jenny put a finger under his chin and forced his mouth closed.

"Ah!" Cat purred as she joined their group, her patrol obviously concluded. "Now I see the appeal. A whole planet and you manage to stumble upon your favorite author, George. What are the odds of that?"

"She's not my *favorite*." George muttered, his own face beginning to flush. "I've read a few of her books though."

"Ha!" Cat snorted as she slid her arm to link with his. "A few. More like all of them!"

"Let it go." George said as he detangled himself and then draped an arm over Jenny's shoulder.

Leela's head swiveled back and forth between the pair, her eyes wide with fascination before settling on the arm now draped over Jenny. A grin broke out on her face, and she gave Jenny a wink. Cat's face contorted to one of anger at the action and she stomped away from the group.

"She doesn't like me very much." Jenny stated, not entirely unaware of the cause of her dislike.

"Don't take it personally. She doesn't like anybody." George replied.

"She likes *you*!" Leela said with the grin still plastered on her face.

"Not interested." George stated emphatically while tucking Jenny closer beneath his arm.

With that subject firmly closed, Leela showed them around camp, and they were soon settled into their own spot with cans of food heating over a campfire. Their meal consisted of spam, corned beef hash and canned vegetables, a veritable feast considering. Many people were introduced to them, and their names were quickly forgotten due to the amount of them. Leela seemed to know everybody and was comfortable with all from both species.

After eating, Nathan soon joined the other children in their play and again Jenny's chest tightened as the remnants of the last few days seemed to fade away and he once again became the laughing, bubbly child that he had been. George and Jenny shared a smile as his tinkling laugh echoed throughout the clearing.

"He seems happy." George said as he pulled Jenny down to sit beside him at the fire.

"He always was. Before. Even when our parents died it couldn't take this from him for long. It is just in his nature. It is one of the things that I admire the most about him. I admit that I didn't know him very well before he came to live with me, but the times that I had seen him he was just as bubbly."

"Why didn't you know him very well?" George asked quietly as if he sensed the sensitivity behind her statement.

"To be honest, my parents and I did not get along very well. They scoffed at my career and no matter how successful I was, it was never enough. To them, writing was a hobby. To me, it was my passion. I couldn't see myself happy doing anything else."

"You do it well. Very well."

"Thank you." She replied with a blush. "I am still a little bit surprised that you have read my books. Even more that you enjoyed them."

George began to flush as well. Even among his species it was unheard of for a man to find pleasure in the romance novels that she had written, and he had so much enjoyed. It wasn't so much the romance aspect that he enjoyed, although that was an added and secret joy, for him it was her writing style. The way that she spun her words allowed him to visualize even the smallest of details as if he were seeing it in a movie in his head.

She had a talent for words that he envied on some levels. Intelligence was something that he admired in an individual and she had it in spades. Hers was a subtle but very much there intelligence that awed and attracted him. In truth, she attracted him more than anybody he had ever met. Even before actually meeting her. It seemed a bit kismet to him that he should happen to find her on this planet out of all the individuals he could have found.

When he had taken on this "mission" his intention was to save as many humans as possible from the fate that awaited them. After meeting her and her brother, that intention had changed. It was imperative to him that they survive. They had, in the short time that he had known them, become his purpose and a necessity in his life. He felt like his very breath depended on their survival. The feeling terrified and excited him simultaneously.

Detracting himself from his worrisome thoughts, George focused his attention back to the smiling and laughing Nathan. The change in the boy was so dramatic and unexpected that he was stunned. Gone was the silent, sullen child that he had initially met. In its place was pure sunshine that a person wanted to get closer to if only to banish the darkness in himself. His very presence was a balm to the soul. He was gravity in living form.

Rising to his feet, he joined Nathan and the other children in a mock wrestling match. His laughter joined theirs as the children mobbed him as one and took him to the ground in a swarm of squirming, squiggling bodies. His stomach soon ached from his laughter, and the amusement of the spectators in camp buoyed his spirits to greater heights.

Still laughing, he latched onto Nathan and pulled him into a bear hug, swinging them both around as if to protect his ward from being touched. Nathan beamed at him, obviously honored by the special attention.

"He's good with kids, isn't he?" A silken voice asked

quietly in Jenny's ear as she admired the sight of children and man playing before her.

"Yes, he is." She agreed warily as she awaited the barb that she was sure would come.

Cat, the owner of the voice was not a fan of her, and she couldn't imagine what slight she had given the woman. It was perplexing to say the least.

"How do you do that?" Jenny asked, "How do you move so silently?"

Cat's only reply was a shrug of indifference. Her cat-like eyes narrowed on Jenny as if she was studying a specimen on display and then shrugged again.

"I don't get it. I have tried to get that man's attention for years. Even signed up on this ridiculous crusade to be near him and he shuns me. But you, he just looks at you and he glows. I just don't get it. What do you have that I don't?"

Ah, Jenny thought, *now we are getting to the heart of the matter!* Cat was *jealous*! That realization awed Jenny. Sitting next to her was one of the most beautiful women that she had ever met, and she was jealous of *her*!

"I honestly don't know. Proximity?" Jenny hedged uncomfortably. "We have been through a lot in a very short amount of time."

"No, that's not it." Cat's voice dripped with disgust. "I am prettier, more seductive, far more intelligent, and yet, he prefers you. It will be different when we get back to our own planet though. He will finally see me when you aren't there to get in the way. He *will* be mine!"

"I am not returning to our planet." George's husky voice interjected, startling both women who had not seen his approach. "I go where Jenny and Nathan go."

"And where is that?" Jenny asked flippantly, irritated again at his lack of answers and partly at her defensive backing against the beautiful Cat. "When?"

"You haven't told her!" Cat crowed in obvious delight.

"Let it go, Cat." George warned.

"*Let it go, Cat.*" She mocked as she walked away shaking her head in disgust.

Chapter 26

George walked off into the woods with the intention of relieving his full bladder in privacy. After finding a deserted area not far from camp, he made quick work of his business and was zipping his pants when he felt a hand caress his back.

Surprised at the silent approach, he turned to see Cat standing behind him. She grinned a seductive smile at him and wrapped her arms around his middle, hugging him to her.

"George, we have been friends for so long." she purred. "Come back home with me. We could be good together."

Her hand slid up his chest in an affectionate gesture, and he gently grabbed her hand to stop the action.

"I don't think of you that way, Cat." he replied, politely ignoring the "friend" comment. His recollection of their history together was quite different. "I am staying with Jenny and Nathan.

"But would she want to stay with *you* if she knew the

truth?" she inquired mockingly. "You really should be honest with her. It's not fair to keep her in the dark."

"If you were her, would you want to know that your world was ending and that nothing would be the same? I am trying to protect her." he replied defensively.

George disentangled himself from Cat's clutching arms and began to walk back to camp when a movement ahead caught his eye. Dread consumed him as he watched a head of blonde hair scurrying away. Inside, he knew that the head belonged to Jenny. *Fuck!* He thought to himself as he hurried after her. *I'm in for it now.*

"Tell her or I will!" Cat yelled in warning to his retreating back.

***

Inside, Jenny seethed in anger and embarrassment at the sight of Cat snuggled up in George's arms. She swallowed a lump in her throat and hurried back toward camp. Tears began to threaten to pool in her eyes, and she forced them back.

She did not get very far when George's firm grip latched on to her arm and spun her around. She had to admire his speed.

"Jenny," he began. "That was not what it looked like. I promise you."

"What was it then? Because you two looked awfully cozy together." she snapped in anger.

"We were just talking." He replied.

"In each other's arms." She stated indignantly.

"She got a little too friendly. I corrected her." He admitted. "I only want you, Jenny."

***

George pulled her into his arms and held her close. After long minutes, he felt her begin to relax into him, and he nearly let out a groan of relief. He knew that he had been forgiven.

A while later, George entered the machine after volunteering for the next patrol after the uncomfortable confrontation with Cat and Jenny. He understood Jenny's inquisitive mind and knew that she deserved answers to all her questions, but he knew that the truth would be a hard pill to swallow, and he didn't want to be the one to bring the pain to her that it would cause. He also knew that was selfish of him.

Slamming his fist into the console as he settled into the seat brought no relief. He felt like he was damned if he did, damned if he didn't, and it wasn't a position he was familiar or comfortable with.

Cat was certainly no help with her continued stirring of the pot. But that was Cat. As much as she liked to think he had not noticed her over the years, he had, and not in a positive light. She had demonstrated over the years how selfish, petulant, and self-serving she could be.

Combined, it was an unattractive element that he was repulsed by. Her outward appearance was all that a man could want, but her inner beauty was non-existent and marred the image in his mind and heart.

Jenny, on the other hand stirred emotions in him that he had not experienced before, and while he welcomed and embraced them, they terrified the hell out of him as well.

She didn't possess the outward beauty that his race readily displayed. Hers was a quiet display that snuck up on a man and stuck. She was not vain, coy, or have any of the other personality traits that so many of his race possessed. She was imperfect perfection.

Powering up the large, familiar machine, he started his patrol scanning left to right, right to left in search of survivors or opposition. Easily, he weaved the machine through the tree lines as comfortable with it as if it was a second skin. A second skin he was ready to shed for the rest of his life.

Damned interfering Cat, he inwardly raged. Her interference could cost him a future that he suddenly wanted so badly that the thought of not having it made him physically ache. Absently, he rubbed at his chest over his heart as if to ease the ache that blossomed there.

For the first time in his life, George had a direction, a destination. He would give up anything and everything to link his life to that of Jenny and Nathan's.

With automatic familiarity, he began to scan the area again for escaped and foe. His machine extremities thundered over the silence as he moved in a wide perimeter around camp. Slowly, very slowly, he inspected his surroundings. All seemed quiet and unnervingly still.

George's skin prickled as a sense of foreboding washed over him. He couldn't understand why he suddenly felt uneasy, but he was never one to ignore his instincts. Something wasn't right and he could feel it.

Tensing in his seat, George turned to make another loop around the perimeter of camp. Trees and bushes surrounded him as he weaved his way through them. *There is nothing*, he thought in frustration.

Sweat beaded on his forehead and he wiped it away with the back of his hand as he decided to head back to camp and hand over patrol to the next volunteer. The feeling of unease grew, and he was practically vibrating with it.

One more scan to the left and he spotted a giant glint of metal. Warning bells rang in his head, and he almost sighed in relief. Turning his machine, he headed toward the threat as his heart began to pound in his chest.

As he neared it, the other machine became visible. There should only be one machine in the area, and he was currently occupying it. His com unit began to crackle before a voice became clear.

"Identify yourself!" The voice barked.

George decided to not respond in hopes that the other would assume his com unit was disabled. It was a stall tactic, and one he didn't think would last for long. He could not let the other machine into camp, but he didn't really wish to fight another of his species either. He needed an idea, and he needed one fast.

"Identify yourself!" The voice barked again.

You are really not helping things here. George thought to himself. Both machines faced off and he could see the driver of the other machine through his shield.

The man had short blonde hair and what could be described as a "pretty boy face" that was typical of their species. Dark eyes matched the equally dark scowl that adorned his face.

For long moments, both men stared at each other, neither blinking, and George resigned himself to the fact that there was not going to be a civil way to end this. Breaking the stalemate, the other man blinked and then pointed toward the exit of the machine, indicating he wanted a face-to-face confrontation.

George nodded at the other man and after powering down his machine, and hearing the other do the same, he prepared to exit. As he approached the other man, a few things occurred to him. The first was that the other man was bigger than he was. A lot bigger. He was taller by half a foot and a lot broader than he was. The second thing that occurred to him was that this man was not going to be easy to take down.

"What are you doing in my sector?" The other man growled out through gritted teeth.

"Patrolling." George answered vaguely with a grin and a shrug that was *not* appreciated by the other man. Humor was obviously beyond this one he thought grimly as he noticed his opponent clench his big beefy fists in irritation.

"Get back in your machine and turn yourself around. This is *my* sector." he ground out angrily.

"Sorry, no can do." George replied flippantly.

The other man's face turned beet red as his anger rose and his fists clenched and unclenched at his sides. His shoulders drew back, and George knew he would not be able to push him much further before he snapped. It wasn't the best plan, but pushing the larger man out of control just might give George the advantage he needed.

"*Why* are you patrolling my sector?" he growled aggressively.

"Because it's my job." George replied with another shrug.

"I am not sharing my kills with you! This sector is mine!" The other man yelled as he stepped closer to George, nearly toe to toe with him now.

"I wasn't aware we were counting." George replied

nonplussed by the invasion of his personal space, and sarcasm dripping from his tone. "How many do you have?"

"Enough. I can add you to the list if you are so anxious to join."

"No, sorry, that wasn't on the agenda for today. But thanks!" George couldn't help but laugh at the outrage on his face as he grew angrier and angrier.

"You are pissing me off man. Get back in your machine and get out of my sector. You are holding me up from my rounds. If you don't move your ass in the next minute, I am going to make you and it's going to hurt."

"I am sorry," George said with a mock apology. "But this sector is mine now. I am afraid you are going to have to leave. See, while you are counting kills, my goal is protection."

"You are a traitor!" he yelled with realization and raised his fist with obvious intent of pummeling George.

This is going to hurt George thought to himself as he decided to allow a single punch, if only to assuage his guilt over having to kill a fellow member of his species.

It was unavoidable and he knew it. This man had to die to protect the people in the clearing, most especially Jenny and Nathan. He could not allow him to either kill them himself or report their location.

Although George had expected the right hook that slammed into his jaw, he had not anticipated the force of it. He staggered briefly from the blow and lights flashed behind his eyes before he quickly recovered himself. He was not fast enough in his recovery, however, and took a second blow to the other side of his jaw.

Determined to not be the only one suffering, George landed a punch of his own to the man's gut and was pleased at the grunt of pain he heard as the man doubled over before righting himself. This further enraged his opponent and George grinned as he knew a complete lack of control was on the horizon.

The man was larger and in a fair fight could probably win this battle. But where he had the brawn, George had a quick wit that he was sure would make him the victor. He just needed to keep him angry enough that he reacted without thinking.

Fists raised, the men circled each other sizing up their opponents and plotting their next moves. Neither struck for a long minute and George worried his adversary was regaining some of his control. His suspicions were confirmed when the man showed his first grin, and George decided another taunt or two was in order.

"Is that all you have then? Now you just intend to dance with me? I'm sorry. You aren't really my type. I prefer soft, willing women to arrogant, ugly assed bastards."

This got the reaction he wanted, and he ducked at the last minute as the next brutal swing headed for his head. The near miss threw his opponent off balance, and he stumbled into a tree before spinning around, not willing to give George the opportunity to take advantage.

"I think you need more dance lessons." George taunted.

"I was just going to beat you bloody, but I've changed my mind." The man spat in reply. "I'm going to end you!"

He pushed off from the tree and lunged at George yet again narrowly missing his prey as he spun his body to the side. George was surprised to find that even though they were in a duel to the death he was beginning to enjoy himself. There was something oddly pleasing being able to thwart a man who could probably crush him if he managed to get his hands on him.

His would-be captor landed on his knees in the dirt and George quickly took advantage as he leaped on his back and locked an arm around the man's throat. Even with his air supply cut off and with the additional weight on his back he managed to stumble to his feet. It was an awkward movement and George had to admire the tenacity until his back was slammed into the nearest tree and he was startled into releasing his grip.

The air was knocked from George's lungs, and he was shrugged off and to the side before the man moved away. Both men bent over coughing and gasping for much needed air. It seemed they were in a bit of a stalemate again which disconcerted George. The man was proving to be a more worthy adversary than he had anticipated, and a nuisance, and he was sick of it.

The man found his breath first and before he could dodge him, George's arm was latched onto, and he was launched into the air and propelled into yet another tree. He hit it hard, and pain screamed in his back at the sudden impact.

Blackness hummed at the edges of his brain, but he forced it aside. Giving in would mean his death and those that he cared about. There would be time to pass out when this was all over. He couldn't give in. He slumped to the ground and waited for the next attack that he was sure would be swiftly arriving.

He was right and felt no shame considering some very dirty tactics. As his attacker rushed within reaching distance, George put all of his strength into his right arm and punched him in the testicles. It had the desired effect and his attacker dropped like a stone and began puking in the grass beside him.

Now in a prone position, and not a current threat to his person, George quickly took the advantage and once again leaped onto him. He straddled him and began slamming his head into the ground repeatedly. He watched as his eyes glazed over with pain and wanted to puke as well. Interesting that he would now notice that his opponent's eyes were an interesting shade of blue. He was sure those eyes would haunt him in his dreams for some time. This level of brutality was beyond him but a necessary evil if he wanted to survive. And he did.

Thinking that he now had the upper hand, George felt a twinge of remorse and relented. He quickly realized his folly as the man's eyes suddenly cleared and he was catapulted off of him and onto the ground beside him and their roles were reversed as the man straddled him.

George didn't see the punch coming but felt and heard the bones in his nose break as the beefy fist slammed into it. Blood sprayed from it and covered the man sitting astride him. The pain was excruciating, and unwelcome tears filled his eyes temporarily blinding him.

"You are going to be my number twenty-seven." The man growled as he wrapped his hands around George's throat.

George tore at the fingers cutting off his airway. Realizing that this action was futile, he forced his arms between his attacker's and yanked them away. The man's weight nearly crushed him as he fell on him with his loss of balance. He let out an oomph at the crushing weight and quickly rolled them over, so he was once again on top. Without hesitation, George grabbed his head and jerked it to the side as far as he could. The man's neck made a sickening snap as it broke, and the breath left his body for the last time.

George rose to his feet on shaky legs and looked down at the prone body.

"One." he said.

Chapter 27

Jenny sat on a log before one of the many fires maintained in the campground with a worn-out Nathan asleep on a blanket at her feet. Playing with the other children in the camp had finally exhausted him and little snores escaped his mouth. He slept the sleep of the innocent and she had to smile at his perseverance. Briefly, she considered moving his blankets further away from the fire, but it was warm, and it felt like they had so little of it lately. It was soothing and she couldn't make herself deprive him of the luxury.

The sunlight was long gone, and the stars were beginning to twinkle in the purplish-blue sky. Absentmindedly, it occurred to her that George had been gone from camp for far longer than she had expected his patrol to last and wondered if he was avoiding her.

She was angry and frustrated with him and she was pretty confident that he knew it. There were things that he was keeping from her, big, life-changing things she was sure, and it both irritated and concerned her that he was unwilling to divulge them.

Grudgingly, she had to admit to herself that his secretiveness wouldn't sting her so much if she hadn't begun to care deeply for the stubborn man. That was a disturbing thought. She had known him for very little time, but she felt like she had known him her entire life. He was obstinate, domineering, and arrogant, but he made her feel safe, cared for, and he was amazingly patient with Nathan.

All around her camp was settling down for the night with the exclusion of "the guardians" as she had begun to call George's species in her mind. They huddled in groups and whispered quietly, but the looks of concern on their faces only added to the apprehension she had begun to feel at George's absence. Her fellow humans seemed oblivious to the tension thickening in the air as time ticked further on. Every once in a while, their gazes flicked to her before quickly turning away before their eyes could meet.

There was definitely something wrong and she could feel it in her bones. A cold burrowed into her that she could not shake despite the warmth of the fire. Apprehension filled her and she rose to join them to demand answers. They would damn well tell her what was going on because this "left in the dark" thing had gone on long enough. Seeking and finding the only familiar face in the bunch, she headed toward "Catty Cat."

Jenny approached quietly and noted that the closer she got, the voices began to silence and one by one, the crowd looked away uncomfortably. *This is not good*, Jenny thought as her heart began to race in her chest, dread flooding her.

Jenny lightly grabbed Cat's arm and was not surprised to feel it tense and recoil under her hand. The woman had an obvious dislike of her although Jenny wasn't quite sure the dislike did not extend to her entire species. She was not sure what had motivated Cat to join the small band of guardians. She suspected that decision had a lot more to do with George than the actual cause.

"Cat?" Jenny asked. "What is going on?"

Cat rolled her eyes and heaved an exaggerated sigh as if answering her was a heavy burden.

"George is missing. He should have been back a long time ago. We are worried something happened to him and our only means of patrol."

The rest of the group scattered as if unwilling to be part of the conversation. Jenny had a feeling it had something to do with her presence.

"Is anybody going to do anything? Go look for him?" Jenny asked, her concern for George growing.

"Wander aimlessly? He could be anywhere!" Cat snorted.

"But he could be in trouble!" Jenny argued, growing annoyed.

"Well obviously!" Cat retorted, her voice dripping with sarcasm. "I'm sure he is not out there picking flowers. Again, we don't know where he is so we wouldn't know where to look. It's a big area to search!"

"So, send scouts in different directions!"

"Your concern is so heart-warming. I've known George a lot longer than you, you know. If it wasn't for him, I wouldn't even be on this god forsaken planet!" Cat hissed at Jenny, baring her pearly white teeth in a sneer of disgust.

"I figured that was the way of it. You don't really like us humans very much, do you?"

"I don't give a crap about your species! That is the way of it! Your species is primitive, inconsequential, and a disgrace to my way of thinking!" Cat spat on the ground at Jenny's feet to demonstrate her opinion.

"Then why are you helping us?"

"Because George is! I have been trying to get his attention for years, but he looks right through me! I thought if I joined his cause he would finally notice me! But instead, he moons over you like you are the very stars in the sky! It disgusts me! I *knew* I should have finished you off at the tunnel!"

A roar of fury filled the air and both women jumped at the sound.

In a flash that was almost too imaginably fast to see, George had Cat by the throat and backed to a tree. Jenny felt a mix of emotions run through her. She was equal parts overjoyed to see that George was back and safe, and equal parts shocked over the revelation that it had been Cat that had tried and almost succeeded in killing them.

Several of their kind ran over to the duo to see what was going on. Confusion was upon all their faces. None seemed inclined to stop George though, and Jenny suspected their loyalty lay with George rather than Cat.

"That was you!?!" George bellowed in her face. "You tried to kill us? *Why*?"

The crowd around them gasped in dismay and sent accusatory looks at Cat. Many looked angry beyond words, and Jenny suspected that if George did not kill her for her betrayal, they just might. Treason was obviously high on their moral offenses and Jenny was oddly admiring that the group stood by a code of honor rather than a code of species.

Cat gurgled unintelligible words in response and George loosened his grip on her throat so that she could speak in defense of herself.

"I didn't know you were in that car."

"And that makes it right!?!" George thundered.

"We had enough people in this wretched camp! We didn't need any more people to pamper and watch over!" Cat whined, a plea in her voice for understanding.

Looking at the faces of all who surrounded them, Cat's eyes pleaded with each one, hoping to find an ally in the group. All she saw in the eyes of her brethren were looks of disgust.

"The point of this mission was to save as many as possible. Not kill them off when we felt we reached an acceptable number. You disgust me. And yes, Cat, I noticed you, and not kindly. I could see the ugliness in you, and I was repulsed by it. Jenny is your complete opposite, and I am grateful for it! Tie this scum to the tree."

George held her to the tree as one of the other men retrieved a rope and did not release her until she had been secured. It was then that his strength waned, and he fell to his knees.

Jenny let out a gasp of surprise and rushed to his side. Only then did she notice his injuries and was appalled by the swelling and bruises on his cheeks, nose and around his eyes.

"George! What happened? Are you okay? Jesus! George, you look horrible!"

At her words of alarm, the group that had been dispelling quickly returned and surrounded them, concern evident in their eyes.

Jenny had not realized before this moment just how important he was to this group. Not only was he part of a close brethren, he was a leader of sorts and their loyalty was finite. She felt a twinge of pride before fear replaced the feeling.

"I had a little run-in." George attempted to joke, but

now that adrenaline was wearing off, the pain in his jaw made it hard to speak.

"Was the situation handled?" Asked one of the men around them and George nodded in affirmation.

"I took care of it and now we have another machine for patrols if someone cares to help me retrieve it."

"There is no need, George." The man replied and the others nodded their agreement. "Point us in the right direction and we will handle it. You just worry about getting yourself fixed up and then rest."

"Out of curiosity, why did it take you so long to return?" Another man inquired and the blush barely visible in the firelight made Jenny curious to hear the answer as well.

"I fainted." George grudgingly admitted and grinned at the few snickers his admission provided. He suspected he would not live that down for a long while.

"I don't think he needs a rest, Gavin." Another man jested to the one who had suggested it. "It appears he already had one!"

Laughter followed the comment and George gave the third man a rude gesture before allowing Jenny to help him to his feet. Jenny led him to the log that she had been sitting on earlier so she could get a better look at his injuries.

"Oh! Your poor face!" She exclaimed in sympathy when she was able to see the full extent of his injuries.

George's cheeks were already black and blue, swollen to look like he was hoarding food in them like a chipmunk. His nose was crooked with dried blood coating a line from his nostrils all the way down to his strong chin, and his eyes were swollen nearly shut and showed signs of an in impending double black eye.

"Not so pretty anymore?" George joked and Jenny couldn't help but giggle at his audacity.

"Not at the moment, but you will heal and be back to being a handsome devil soon enough." She replied sincerely and with affection. "Let me see if I can find some water and a clean rag so we can clean you up. What I wouldn't give for ice right now. At least it would bring some of the swelling down."

"I have a first aid kit." Leela quietly stated, startling them both as they had not heard her approach. "I know there is an ice pack in it and ibuprofen too I believe. I will be right back with the kit and some water."

Jenny latched onto her hand as she began to walk away and gave her a bright smile.

"Thank you, Leela."

As they waited for Leela's return, Jenny noted that George was shifting uncomfortably on the log that he was sitting on and suspected he had far more injuries than she could see.

"Are you alright, George?" she asked in concern.

"It's my back. The bugger slammed me against a tree when I was trying to choke him." he admitted sheepishly.

Jenny had him turn on the log so that his back was to the fire and gingerly helped him remove his shirt so she could see the extent of the injuries to his back. She tried to ignore the blush that heated her cheeks when she realized that he had a very nice back and focus on the bruising that was already formed on it. His back was all corded muscle and as she had suspected, he didn't have an ounce of fat on him. The man was mouth-wateringly handsome in all ways, even with the bruising that ran the length of his spine.

"You are bruised, but there are no cuts. You really took a beating! I hope the other guy looks just as bad!"

"I snapped his neck." George answered honestly and then winced at the realization that he didn't have to be quite so honest. He hoped she was not repulsed.

"Good!" She responded with vigor, surprising him with her ferocity.

Jenny got George turned back around on the log as Leela stepped up beside them with first-aid kit, a jug of water and rags in hand.

"I can reset your nose if you'd like." Leela offered softly. "It will hurt like hell and most likely start bleeding again, but I was a nurse in a not so nice area and have assisted in more than my share of them. Done a few myself."

George considered the offer and although he was

not looking forward to the pain, he also did not want to seem like a wimp in front of Jenny and his men. Grimly, he nodded acceptance and stiffened which caused his bruised back to ache.

"I've got a bottle of whiskey." Gavin stated, joining their small group. "Maybe he should drink some before you set his nose. Might make it a bit more tolerable."

George didn't know what whiskey was, but if it was going to take some of the pain away, he was more than willing to try.

Gavin dropped a bottle of amber liquid into his lap, and he muttered his thanks. Taking a large swig from the bottle, he coughed from the flames that radiated down his throat. Warmth filled his belly, and he took another swig. This one went down much smoother. It tasted like hell, but if it was going to help it was worth the affront on his palette.

"More." Gavin urged, and George took another large swig.

"Not too much," Leela warned, "Or he is not going to remain sitting, and we will have a hell of a time fixing him up without the light."

Gavin grinned and urged George to take another swig, to which he dutifully complied. By the fourth swig, the whiskey didn't taste so bad, and George grinned goofily. A warm buzz flowed through his veins, and he was feeling quite comfortable.

"I think he's ready now." Leela exclaimed, and without warning, she grabbed on to his nose and wrenched it into place.

Even with the whiskey running through his veins and the warmth spread throughout his body, the sudden pain was so extreme that George came up swinging. Before he could injure anyone, Gavin restrained him in a bear hug until the pain eased some and blood poured down his face.

"Give me the bottle." George growled, and Gavin laughed as he released him and handed it to him.

"Hurt just a little?" Gavin asked with humor.

"Like hell." George replied honestly as he took another swig from the bottle and staggered.

Gavin straightened him and Jenny hurriedly laid a blanket out next to the still sleeping Nathan for him to be laid on. Gavin laid him down on his side and Leela and Jenny began to clean his face before applying the ice pack to the cheek that was not burrowed in the blanket.

Jenny was relieved when the blood pouring from his nose finally staunched itself and moved the ice pack to cover his nose and eye. She let out a tear of sympathy at the agony he was feeling but trying so hard to hide and was surprised to feel a soothing hand on her shoulder.

"He will be alright, Jenny." Leela said reassuringly. "Although, he may experience his first hang-over in the morning."

Jenny grinned and silently agreed as his soft snores filled the silence on their camp. She was grateful that there was indeed ibuprofen in the first aid kit because she knew he was going to need some for more than one reason now.

Chapter 28

George woke with a splitting headache to add to the numerous other aches he was able to catalog before he grudgingly opened his eyes to the bright sunlight that shot daggers into his brain. Nausea gripped him and he shut his eyes with haste. The urge to retch was almost overwhelming and he took deep breaths until his stomach ceased churning.

"Here. Take these." Jenny implored him soothingly as she forced a couple of pills between his lips and a cool drink slid down his throat to follow them. "Just lay there for a while and they should help ease your pain."

George grunted in response, feeling incapable of words at that moment. Jenny giggled at the rude gesture, obviously understanding the reasoning behind it. The injuries themselves were nothing to laugh about but she suspected the hangover took precedence over those pains.

"Is he ok?" He heard Nathan's worried voice ask in a whisper.

He cracked an eye open and gave Nathan a crooked smile to reassure him. Settling back on the blanket in as comfortable of a position as he could muster, he waited for the pills that Jenny had given him to kick in and the pain to diminish some.

"He will be fine." He heard Jenny reply in a soothing voice. "Did you see? He smiled at you."

"But his face is all swollen and dark!"

"Just bruising. He will heal and look normal again." Jenny reassured him before shooing him off to play with the other children that had risen.

Food was being handed out by fellow camp mates and Jenny watched as Nathan grabbed his share before running off with the other children. Sure that he would be well watched, she returned her focus to George.

"How are you feeling?"

"Like I got the crap beat out of me." He replied with a grin.

"I can't imagine why you would feel like that." She retorted with a snort. "Do you want to try some food? It might help the hangover."

George inwardly cringed at the thought of food and suspected he would not be ready to eat until his head stopped pounding.

"Not yet, but thanks."

"Well, I will go grab our shares and we can eat when you are ready." she replied.

"You don't have to wait for me."

Jenny tsked at that and he heard her walk away. Feeling bold, he dared to open his eyes a crack and discovered that the stabbing pain had dulled some. It was still there but didn't make him want to vomit all over himself. Deciding to give himself a bit more time for the medicine to do its job, he closed his eyes and found himself dozing.

***

George woke up what felt like a few minutes later but suspected it had actually been longer. He hoped that Jenny had not in fact waited for him.

Stretching proved to be a mistake and the ache in his back made him gasp and wince. The pain in his face throbbed as well but his head had improved, and his stomach growled.

Sitting up, he drew the attention of Jenny who had been resting on the log beside him watching the children play. She smiled at him, and he returned the gesture as best as he could with a sore jaw.

"How are you feeling? Is your head better now?"

"Much. It's my face and back that hurt now. How long was I out?"

"Only about an hour," she replied with a shrug. "Are you hungry?"

"Very." He responded with a grin.

"Good! I saved you a large portion of oatmeal. I figured you would need something that didn't require chewing."

His heart clenched at her thoughtfulness. She really was the most perfect woman he had ever met. He doubted any other would have considered the pain that chewing would cost him. Even talking hurt.

"Leela stopped by earlier while you were napping with another ice pack. Someone else had a first aid kit as well. That should take some of the swelling down. I'm just not sure where you need it the most. Your cheeks and nose are swollen, and you look like a racoon."

George tried to remember what the animal looked like but couldn't place it. His interests were leaned toward the more predatory animals like lions, cheetahs and bears. He had to imagine a racoon was not a very appealing looking creature though if her grimace was any indication.

George hastily ate his oatmeal which abated his gnawing hunger. It had not been easy to eat since it still required constant movement of his jaw. He let out a sigh of contentment though and accepted the ice pack that Jenny had cracked and handed to him when she noted that he had finished.

He felt silly sitting on the blanket with an ice pack pressed to his cheek, occasionally switching sides. Jenny moved to sit next to him, and they watched the children in companionable silence.

The children had evidently opted for a game of

hide-and-go-seek which was a bit laughable as the only places they had to hide were behind people or trees and their giggles gave them away more times than not.

George and Jenny shared a grin as they watched Nathan's turn as "the seeker." The boy counted with his hands over his eyes, fingers spread so he could watch the flurry of children run and hide.

"He's a cheat." Jenny laughed, and George nodded his agreement.

Squeals of laughter filled the air as he "found" the other children. George closed his eyes in contentment at the sound. *This* was what they had been working so hard to save. The innocence and caring of these people did not deserve to be snuffed out. It angered him that his own species felt it was their right and their duty to do so. He was glad and honored that he was not alone in his beliefs.

Putting this mission together had not been easy and was not as well planned as he would have liked. He wished that they could have saved far more of the humans but were forced into making a hasty plan once word reached him that they would be annihilated.

A whisper in this ear and another could have cost him his life, but he had felt it was worth the cost, and he was surprised when this small group of people flocked to his door and a plan was formed. It was a simple plan. They would all ride along, pretending to be part of the units, save as many as they could, and meet at their designated extraction point.

They had one of their men, who was a captain who would extract them all at a specific time. All under the nose of their home base. It was a risky plan, but worth it if they succeeded. They just needed to wait a couple more days and it would all be over.

George's thoughts were interrupted as he watched Gavin approach with a wide, mischievous grin on his face. He knew that some kind of ribbing was headed his way and he groaned.

"Good morn." Gavin said in a mock Scottish brogue that he had perfected if only because it amused him. "And how is the wee lad this morning?"

"The wee lad is fine." George replied while rolling his eyes and switching the ice pack to his other cheek.

"Is this bonnie lass taking good care of you then, laddie?" he asked, winking at Jenny who began to blush at the comment.

"Yes." George responded in aggravation. "What do you want, Gavin? Besides the honor of embarrassing my woman?"

The claim of ownership was not lost on Gavin, and he smiled brightly. It was obvious that he approved of the relationship between George and Jenny.

"Well," Gavin started in his normal voice. "I thought I would let you know we are making use of that second machine and rounds have doubled. So far there have been no new arrivals or opposition. Also, Cat is not very happy being tied to the that tree. She is whining to anybody who walks by that she is hungry and needs to relieve herself. Do we untie her?"

"We shouldn't give her the luxury since she doesn't have a care for our cause and the people we are saving, but yes. Put a female guard on her and when she is done her business, tie her back up. We can't allow her to escape and report our location. Tell whoever you pick as guard to not leave her side and expect trickery. Have a male guard follow the pair at a distance as backup."

"You really think she will try to overpower one of her own kind to escape?" Gavin asked in surprise.

"I have no doubt."

Jenny tensed beside him, and he instinctively put an arm around her shoulders and gave her an affectionate squeeze. Gavin's smile broadened even more at the show of fondness, and he walked away to carry out his orders.

"Do you really think she would harm one of her own kind just to get away?" Jenny whispered as she leaned closer into his warm embrace.

"It would not surprise me." He replied as he pulled her even closer to his side. "Cat has always been first and foremost about Cat. Her wants always take precedence. To be honest, I was surprised when she had joined our mission. It seemed very out of character, and I should have been wary of her reasons. But at the time, I was just happy to have one more person to help."

"What are you saving us from, George? What are you trying so hard to not tell me?"

"Not today, Love. I will explain to you as much as I don't want to, but not today. Let's enjoy one peaceful day. We have earned it."

Jenny was so stunned by the term of endearment that she couldn't rouse the anger that usually accompanied his deflections of the truth. Her heart warmed and she easily agreed to the one day of freedom from the troubles that had surrounded them. She rested her head on his shoulder, and he took that as a sign of affirmation.

Jenny had to stifle a giggle as Nathan came barreling their way and quickly ducked behind George. Her would-be giggle soon turned to concern as she saw the grimace on George's face. She quietly warned the boy to be careful around his back since it was sore, and Nathan crawled back a bit with an apologetic look on his face.

"Sorry." Nathan whispered in George's ear.

Not being able to respond with waves of pain radiating throughout his spine, George just nodded at the boy and took deep breaths until the waves of pain began to dull.

Nathan was quickly discovered, and the game resumed as he ran off again. The restful silence resumed, and Jenny and George enjoyed the quiet company they brought each other. Neither felt the need to talk and both were glad of it. They needed this faux paradise time to help erase the days of the past and the shaky ones of the future.

Minutes later, a flurry of activity among his people drew his attention and he cursed under his breath as a shrieking Cat was carried back into the clearing. He had been right to assume she would try *something*. With a groan, he heaved himself to his feet and followed the procession to the tree that they had originally tied her to.

Once again, Cat was secured to her tree, and she screamed in fury. None of her words made sense, even to her own kind because she spat them out so quickly and with a pitch that would make anyone cringe. Others around her covered their ears and winced. George was tempted to join them.

"I want to talk to George!" Cat yelled in a more tolerable pitch and inwardly, George groaned. *There goes my peaceful day*, he thought.

Chapter 29

George approached Cat with an audible groan. His face and back were aching and the last thing he wanted to do was deal with her and her crap. She smiled at him as he neared, and he wondered what she was playing at now. Whatever it was, he did not have the patience for it.

"George," She cooed, "You aren't really going to leave me tied to this tree all day, are you? I've learned my lesson. I want to help."

"I'm not falling for your act, Cat. You nearly killed me, Jenny and Nathan, and you would have killed anybody coming out of that tunnel. You don't deserve freedom. I gave you a chance to see to your needs and you tried to flee and injured one of your own kind. No, Cat. I don't care if you urinate or crap yourself. You are staying tied to the tree. So, you might as well settle in and get comfortable."

"But George," she whined.

"Save it, Cat." George growled, cutting her off.

He started to walk away when her screeches had him

turning around and heading back to her. He looked at her and then to Gavin who was lounging against a tree watching the debacle.

"Gag her."

"Will do." Gavin replied with a grin.

George started walking back toward Jenny and their makeshift camp site when he heard a slapping sound and Gavin yelling about Cat biting him. He didn't turn around this time though. He spotted Jenny sitting on the log and sat beside her.

"Everything alright?" Jenny asked.

"It is now. Cat thought she would con me into releasing her. Instead, she's tied to the tree again with a gag in her mouth. She won't be bothering anybody else today."

Jenny was surprised by this side of George but inwardly shrugged. His kind had their own code, and she wasn't in a position to argue it.

Peals of laughter drew their attention and they turned to watch children race by them. Once the last child passed them, warning bells began to ring in Jenny's head. Quickly, she rose to her feet and began scanning the camp.

"George, I don't see Nathan."

"What?" he asked as he rose to stand next to her.

"I don't see Nathan anywhere." Jenny replied, fear creeping into her voice.

George lightly grabbed the arm of the next child to

run by and asked if he knew where Nathan was. After shaking his head, the boy ran off to join the other kids.

"I'm sure he is fine." George said in as reassuring a tone as he could muster. "I will grab some guys and we will search for him. He couldn't have gone far. Stay here in case he comes back, okay?"

Jenny nodded and he bent to kiss her forehead. It was a sweet, endearing gesture but did little to calm her nerves. Looking at George's battered face made her shiver in fear. Nathan was too little to be able to defend himself. Not that there was a guarantee there was another out there like the one that George fought. But there was no guarantee there wasn't either.

She watched as George rounded up volunteers, most of the helpers of his own kind, including Gavin. After speaking with them for a minute, they all departed in different directions calling Nathan's name.

***

Jenny tried not to let her fear overtake her and she sat roughly on the log to wait. An arm came around and over her shoulder in a comforting touch and she looked to see Leela standing next to her.

"I'm sure they will find him soon enough. And I do not envy that boy when they find him. I think he's going to get a whole round of scoldings."

"He has a tendency to wander." Jenny sighed in

exasperation. "He is very little and doesn't understand the danger. Although I wish he would! It has been hell lately and as much as I don't want to curb his enthusiasm for life, I wish he would show more caution."

"Oh, once George gets hold of him, I'm sure he will." Leela chuckled. "Not that I think George would hurt him. But it's obvious that Nathan looks up to him. I think one look of disappointment and that will be that."

"I hope you are right." Jenny sighed. "Or that boy is going to be tied up right next to Cat."

Jenny scooted over on her log so Leela could sit next to her, and they listened to voices calling Nathan's name in the distance and waited.

***

George walked as straight of a line as he could with Gavin 10 paces away. They dodged trees and bushes and straightened back out as best as they could while trying to stick to their plots. Instinct told George he was headed in the right direction, but he couldn't be sure.

A chorus of "Nathan" could be heard from all directions. It sounded loud amongst the eerie silence, and he cringed. If there was another machine out there, they were all making themselves easy targets. All because of one boy that liked to wander. George ran his hands through his hair in frustration and called out to the boy.

"We will find him." Gavin called out to him. "And

then you can give him hell and turn him over to his sister so she can too."

George did not have a polite response to his friend's comment, so he grunted and kept walking. He had known Gavin for many years, and he was one of the few people that he considered a friend. They complimented each other with their conflicting personalities.

George was the more serious of the two, whereas Gavin was a prankster with a goofy sense of humor. Gavin was able to find humor in any situation and it was a trait that George admired. Perhaps even more so as he had been developing a lightness and sense of humor since he met Jenny and Nathan.

They had been on many hunts together on various planets saving as many of the life forces as they could. The pair had mastered the art of communication without words and could read each other better than most. George was glad to have him by his side.

Both men continued walking and shouting for Nathan. During one of the silences, George thought he heard a small giggle and stopped. Out of the corner of his eye he noted that Gavin had stopped as well.

"Nathan?" George called out while looking around him.

Another giggle came in response, and he ground his teeth in frustration. He could not pinpoint where the giggle was coming from.

"Nathan, this is not funny. Come out now."

Another giggle followed and Gavin let out a short whistle to grab his attention and pointed upward with his head. George looked up into the tree that Gavin had indicated and spotted a little head peeking down at him from high up in the branches. Relief warred with anger when he spotted the boy.

"Come down from there, Nathan." George said quietly, not wanting to startle the boy with his anger.

Gavin, George noted, had moved himself directly under Nathan, presumably to catch him if he fell. As Nathan maneuvered his way around and down, Gavin moved to match his position.

Once Nathan reached the lowest and thickest branch, he realized that getting down was far more difficult than it had been to get up and let out a cry of fear.

"I can't get down, George." Nathan whined, his lower lip wobbling.

George sighed and moved to stand in front of the boy and raised his arms to him. He was still high and out of reach, but George could easily catch him at that distance.

"Come on then." George said and Nathan shook his head at him.

"You'll drop me."

"Never." George stated emphatically and realized that he meant it.

As frustrating as the boy could be, George would

always be there for him. Nathan reached for George and dropped out of the tree into his waiting arms.

"Found him!" Gavin called out loudly and a chorus of "found" could be heard throughout the woods. This had been their predetermined signal for all to return to the safety of camp.

George lowered Nathan to the ground and gripped his shoulders in a tight hold. The boy was still trembling in fear, but he could not allow that to deter him.

"What were you thinking wandering off like that?" George snarled at him.

"I was playing hide-and-seek." Nathan replied in a whisper-soft voice.

"Do you realize that you endangered the *entire camp* with this stunt? Look at my face, Nathan. This could have happened to anybody that had to stop to search for you. Or our camp could have been discovered as we called out for you, and we would all be in danger. You need to *think*, boy!"

"I'm sorry, George." Nathan sniffled, tears welling in his eyes. "I just wanted to play."

Reminded once again how very young Nathan was, George pulled him in for a tight hug. The relief he felt at finding Nathan alive and well mingled with the lingering anger he felt, and he tried to force the anger aside.

"George." Gavin admonished in a gentle voice, and no further words were needed.

George reined in his anger and steered the boy back to their camp and his very worried, most likely panicked sister. They walked side-by-side, the only sound being the leaves that crunched under their feet.

Chapter 30

Jenny let out a cry of relief as she heard the chorus of "found him" surrounding their camp and waited anxiously for the sight of her little brother. She felt like a failure as a mother figure but decided to worry about that emotion later. She just wanted him safe in her arms before she tore into him for his stupidity.

Minutes later, volunteers began to trickle back into the camp and Leela squeezed her hand in support as they waited to see the little troublemaker.

As George, Nathan and Gavin entered the clearing, Jenny let out a sigh of relief and rose to greet them. Nathan's chin was almost touching his chest with his head down and Jenny suspected George had already had a "talk" with the boy.

Gavin and Leela wandered off and George stood there watching as Jenny hugged her brother and then raised his face to give him a stern look.

"Nathan, what were you thinking?" Jenny asked. "You can't just go wandering off!"

"I know, Sissy. I'm sorry. I just wanted to play." he responded, tears welling in his eyes. "I climbed really high in a tree though. Really, really high."

"Nathan!" she responded in exasperation. "You are not getting it. It is not safe to leave this campground! Do it again and I am going to tie you to the tree next to Cat! Is that what you want?"

Nathan looked properly horrified at the threat and shook his head vigorously. George had to stifle a laugh at the expression on the boy's face. He knew that it was an idle threat, but the boy obviously did not.

"Go and play. But stay where you can be seen!" Jenny dismissed her ward with another stern look of authority. He didn't have to be asked twice and ran off to join the other children.

Jenny leaned into George as the boy ran off and rested her head on his shoulder. He put an arm around her in a comforting embrace and gently squeezed.

"Thank you, George." She whispered.

George grunted in response, apparently feeling the thanks unnecessary, and began to walk them back to their campsite. He suspected all the camp dwellers would be keeping a much closer eye on the little rascal they had to hunt down. As they made their way to their campsite, he nodded his thanks to the volunteers they passed. Many nodded back and others just grinned.

As they passed a still-tied Cat, she snarled at them, her gag around her throat. She had obviously managed to finagle it from her mouth.

"Lost the little brat, did you?" she taunted Jenny.

"Lost your little bladder, did you?" Jenny taunted back indicating the wet urine stains that covered the front of her pants.

George had been about to intervene when Jenny lashed back at Cat, and he had to admire her grit. Jenny had some claws of her own. He bit back a laugh and urged her onward. The sound of Cat's indignant retorts trailed them, and he gave in to the urge to laugh.

When they reached their campsite, George drew Jenny in for a hug, still laughing.

"My kitty has claws!" he exclaimed with a chuckle.

"When someone raises my temper, yes." She replied with an adorable blush. "You'd do well to remember that mister."

"I will keep that in mind." He said with mock seriousness.

They sat next to each other on their blanket and watched as the children played and some of their fellow refugees began to prepare a lunch fare for the entire group.

"I should offer to help them." Jenny remarked and

started to rise only to have George grasp her hand and pull her back down on the blanket next to him.

"They've got it handled. Keep me company." He replied. "I just got the crap beat out of me recently, you know. I could use the sympathy."

Jenny snorted at his ploy for sympathy but settled more comfortably next to him.

"Your face doesn't look nearly as swollen today. Is healing quickly one of your traits?" she inquired.

"I wouldn't know." He replied honestly with a shrug. "I have no way of judging how quickly one of your kind would heal from that. I'm healing as quickly as I should."

"Then you definitely heal faster because I would still be swollen and bruised for days."

George didn't like thinking about the idea of Jenny suffering the attack that he had, and it made his protective instincts flare to life.

"I would never let someone hurt you like that." He stated emphatically.

"I know you wouldn't." she said soothingly.

Mollified, he turned back to surveying the campsite. Jenny leaned into his side, and he wrapped a protective arm around her. The sweet gesture made her smile and a warm, fuzzy feeling fluttered in her belly.

"Are you really going to leave Cat tied to a tree?" Jenny asked quietly.

"Yes. She is a danger to all. I won't risk the safety of

everybody to spare one person the embarrassment she now feels. Tomorrow she will receive the punishment she deserves for her treachery."

"Isn't sitting in her own urine and God knows what punishment enough? What…"

"She had intended murder, Jenny." He replied with a growl. "Where I come from, that is a capital offense. We are the Guardians and live by a very strict code."

"What will you do with her?" she asked.

"She will be left behind." He responded gruffly.

"Left behind?" Jenny asked with a whisper. "What does that mean? Are we moving camp tomorrow?"

"Enough questions!" George snapped, evasive as always before looking at her apologetically. "I'm sorry. My head is pounding. Could we sit quietly for a bit?"

"Yes. I'm sorry." Jenny said with concern in her voice. "Do you need anything?"

George didn't answer but rose and stomped off toward the woods. He didn't look back and Jenny was stunned by his behavior. His hot to cold attitude was perplexing.

"He won't tell you; you know." Cat's voice called out in a sing-song voice. "But I will."

Chapter 31

"What is he hiding?" Jenny asked as she approached a grinning Cat. "What doesn't he want me to know?"

"Have a seat." She replied, nodding to the grass in front of her.

"I'll stand, thank you."

Cat shrugged her shoulders and leaned back into the tree. Her grin widened, and a mischievous twinkle lit her eyes making them appear even more cat-like. Her expression reminded Jenny of the Cheshire cat from Alice in Wonderland.

"You are not moving camp. You are moving planets."

"What?" Jenny gasped at the bold statement.

"Want to sit down now?" Cat snickered and Jenny dropped into the grass with an oomph.

"Why would we be moving planets?" Jenny asked quietly.

"Your planet is dying, you idiot. Surely you noticed

that." Exasperation dripped from Cat's voice, and she looked at Jenny as though she was a naïve child.

"Well the tornadoes.." Jenny started to reply before trailing off.

"No." Cat corrected her. "Those were us. We needed a distraction so we could land without being seen. And it worked too, didn't it?"

"I don't understand."

"The tornadoes were us. A distraction. The gravity was us. We needed to reclaim all of the wildlife for relocation and filter out your species. Our machines were to take care of the rest of your species. Complete annihilation."

"But *why*?" Jenny asked, perplexed.

"This is not the first time we bailed your species out." Cat sighed in exasperation. "Your species killed the original Earth and were placed here with the understanding that history would not repeat itself. And yet, it did. Earth 2.0 is almost as bad off as the original Earth now."

"Earth 2.0? What is going to happen to this planet?"

"By this time tomorrow, this planet won't exist. It will be turned into stardust." Cat grinned maliciously.

Jenny gaped in dismay over the pending destruction of her home. She felt like the moment was surreal, but with the recent events, not unthinkable. Her breath came in fast pants, and she thought she might hyperventilate. This was too much for her to handle, and she suspected this was the reason George had been so evasive with his answers.

"I need some air." Jenny said as she staggered to her feet. It was a ludicrous statement, but her brain was on overload with too much information, and thinking of something intelligent to say was too much effort.

The sound of Cat's laughter followed her as she walked away. With no destination in mind, she wandered away from camp. She didn't want to be around other people now and wasn't even sure if the others were aware of what was going to happen. That was information she had no desire to share. The knowledge was too much of a burden.

Jenny wandered further into the woods for a few minutes before stopping at the sound of leaves crunching behind her. She froze in place, filled with terror as she waited to discover if the intruder was friend or foe.

***

George came upon Jenny and was stunned by the look of sheer terror plastered on her face. His heart clenched at the sight, and he was grateful that soon it would be all over and she would be safe.

"It's okay, Jenny. It's just me. You are safe."

"Am I really?" she replied, her voice dripping with sudden anger and frustration.

"She told you. Damn it! I didn't want you to know!"

He snarled as he slammed a fist into the tree beside him. "I didn't want you to be afraid! I was trying to protect you!"

George pulled her into his arms and cradled her head on his chest. Stroking her hair, he was silent until he felt her relax in his arms.

"Your people are going to destroy the Earth?" she questioned his neck in a whisper.

George sat, pulling her into his lap as he thought of how to answer her in a way that would alleviate her fears.

"Yes. But it's not what you think. This planet is dying. It will be destroyed with the hope that it will be recycled into a new sustainable planet. My kind are not monsters. We are Guardians."

"But your kind wants to eradicate my entire species!"

"Ah. That." He sighed. "Not all of us agree with that decision. Thus, the rescue mission we are risking our lives for. You need to understand the perspective. My kind saved yours once before and with the belief that history would not repeat itself and this planet would be better taken care of. We gave you tools for advancement and somehow instead of advancing, your kind reverted, the message was lost, and we are back to square one. My kind is not very forgiving."

"Tools for advancement?"

"The pyramids, Bermuda triangle, Nazca lines.. I won't go into detail because that would take forever." He replied with a chuckle.

"It hardly seems fair to eradicate an entire species because a message was lost throughout centuries. Have you ever heard of whisper down the lane? The message rarely ends as it began." Jenny huffed indignantly, causing George to chuckle again.

"*You* are going to survive. Nathan is going to survive. The entire camp and the other camps all around the world are going to survive. We could not save all of mankind, but we are saving as many as we can."

George pulled her close and hugged her tightly, sharing his warmth and comfort with her. She was silent for a few minutes absorbing the new information he had imparted.

"George?" Jenny asked, "Where will we go?"

"Ah." He replied with a grin. "That is the beauty of it. There is a planet that my kind goes to when we want to retire, as your kind calls it. Once you are there, nobody ever leaves. It is the perfect place to relocate you. The planet is primitive by our standards and there would be no way to share the news of our arrival. We will be safe there and can live in peace."

"What is it like there?" she inquired, intrigued by the prospect.

"I don't know. I have never been there. Once my kind goes there, we never return. We will find out together. Come. Let's go back to camp. Tomorrow will be here soon enough."

George stood, helped her to her feet and hand in hand they walked back to camp. The day flew by and soon enough it was nightfall. Jenny, George and Nathan snuggled together on a blanket, although Nathan was the only one that obtained real sleep. Minds wandered and apprehension was abundant.

Morning came quickly and as camp arose, excitement crackled in the air. It was unclear how many of the large party actually knew what was going on, but the cheer was infectious for all but George. He had deliberately withheld the mode of their transportation from Jenny and his conscience was eating at him. His nerves were raw, and he checked the watch-like monitor on his wrist frequently. This action did not go unnoticed by Jenny and she looked at him with concern in her eyes.

"Are you alright? What is going on?" she asked.

George pulled her and Nathan to the outskirts of camp and away from any prying ears.

"There is something that I did not share with you because you are not going to like it. I need you to trust me. In a few minutes, you will be safe, and we will be on our way to our new lives."

"I trust you, George!" Nathan chirped emphatically.

"What is it you haven't told us?" Jenny questioned apprehensively.

"Do you remember when the gravity changed? That is how we will reach the ship. Only this time there will be no filter. Our DNA is too similar to your own and there will be no risking any of our kind. Just hold my hand and trust me to keep you safe. Can you do that?"

Nathan nodded enthusiastically and with a knot in her throat, Jenny did the same. George was used to the kind of transportation they were about to endure and admittedly still found the experience uncomfortable, but he kept his unease to himself and gave the pair a reassuring smile.

Nathan latched onto one of George's hands and Jenny did the same, her knuckles white with a painfully tight grip. He pulled her closer to his side and hoped the contact would help ease her discomfort and fears. A few minutes later a tingling sensation filled the group and silence fell.

"George?" Cat's voice screeched in the silence. "George! You aren't really going to leave me here, are you? George, please! I don't want to die!"

Gravity shifted and the group began to rise. George looked to where Cat was still firmly tied to the tree and felt no sympathy or regret.

"Goodbye, Cat."

Epilogue

Jenny rose from their bed and slipped silently onto the balcony. Looking out over the horizon that was so eerily similar to the one she had been used to her entire life, it was easy to forget that the last year of her life had happened.

After the terrifying transportation to the ship, the rest of the journey was uneventful, and they quickly settled into their new lives together.

Nathan had grown over an entire foot in the last year and had lost some of his wildness. Jenny attributed the change to his admiration of George and his desire to emulate him. He still pulled the occasional prank and still had a fascination with buttons, but he was no longer the carefree spirit he had been.

George had taken a position on the planet council, which suited him. He was solely responsible for passing several mandates that contributed to a peaceful worldwide society of Guardians and humankind.

Jenny continued to write and began to teach English to young children at the local school.

Leaning her elbows on the railing, she listened to the sound of the crickets chirping happily in the background and thought back to the days of horror they had experienced. Those dark days were over now, but if she had learned anything from the experience it was to never forget.

Warm hands surrounded her and rested gently on her severely swollen abdomen. A light kiss fluttered over her cheek, and she smiled with love.

"Couldn't sleep?" George asked, looking up to the 2 moons that glowed brightly in the sky. The moons were the only discernable difference between the planet they had left and the one that they had settled on.

"No. Your children are very active tonight." She said as a kick fluttered in her abdomen.

"I see that." George replied with a chuckle, and he moved his hand to better feel the lives growing with her.

The children had been a surprise. Although in retrospect, they shouldn't have been. Thinking back to crazy Maddie's prophecy, she realized that she had been correct after all. Everything really did come in threes.

"I was just thinking about the last year and all that has happened since tornadoes struck and life turned upside down, sideways and back upright again." Jenny said quietly.

"Well." George stated with all seriousness. "It is a very good thing that at the end, there is always a new beginning."

Acknowledgements

First and foremost, I would like to thank you, the reader, for taking the time to read my work. I hope that you enjoyed it as much as I enjoyed writing it!

Second, I would like to thank my children for their love and support. They are my greatest achievement in life and my inspiration to keep at it and never give up.

To my family and friends who have supported me and patiently waited for me to accomplish my goal, thank you!

Thank you to Karl for creating the most amazing cover I could have asked for. And a special thank you to Drew for my author photo.

Lastly, thank you to Ron and Mark who listened to me ramble on for hours and hours and allowed me to bounce ideas off of them. You guys are incredible people.

Printed in the United States
by Baker & Taylor Publisher Services